TAURUS

Edited by Austin P. Sheehan

Mikhaeyla Kopievsky & Helena McAuley

THE ZODIAC SERIES

The Zodiac Series is a collection of twelve speculative fiction anthologies, each focusing on one of the Zodiac signs. The anthologies feature short stories and poems inspired by each sign, and retellings of the various myths behind those signs.

\#

Capricorn Aquarius Pisces

Aries Taurus Gemini

Cancer Leo Virgo

Libra Scorpio Sagittarius

\#

The Zodiac Series has been produced by Aussie Speculative Fiction, and each anthology contains a diverse selection of tales by talented writers from Australia and New Zealand.

First published by Deadset Press in 2020.

Cover design Copyright © Austin P. Sheehan.

Edited by Austin P. Sheehan, Mikhaeyla Kopievsky and Helena McAuley.

Foreword by Sasha Hanton.

I AM TAURUS

Zoey Xolton

I am the Bull and my constellation is Taurus

My tarot card is The Hierophant; I am a devoted friend and tactile
individual.

At my best I am reliable, practical and patient.

At my worst I am uncompromising, stubborn and possessive.

Strong and stable, like my element: Earth, mine is a Fixed sign.

I appreciate romance, cooking, gardening and material wealth.

However, I dislike insecurity, complications and sudden change.

I am ruled by Venus, and am guardian to the first and fifth days of the
week.

My colours are pink and green.

About the Author:

Zoey Xolton is an Australian Speculative Fiction writer, primarily of Dark Fantasy, Paranormal Romance, and Horror. Her works have appeared in over one-hundred themed anthologies, with more due for publication! She has recently celebrated the release of her debut short story collection Darkly Ever After. You can find further details regarding her many publications on her website: www.zoeyxolton.com!

Contents

I am Taurus by Zoey Xolton... v

Foreword by Sasha Hanton.. 1

The Bull of Heaven by Alannah K. Pearson.............................. 5

Pleiades by Jenny Blackford 23

The Body in the Wall by Stephen Herczeg.............................. 25

Meet Me by the Moon When I'm Flicking Through a Cheap Magazine Talking about Astrology by Brianna Bullen 59

The Taurean by Austin P. Sheehan 71

A Tale of Hearts and Horns by Nikky Lee............................... 77

Tercio de Muerte by BG Hilton.. 109

The Eternal Twilight of His Maze by Jenny Blackford 113

Displeasure of the Gods by P.A. Mason 127

Lord Apis by BG Hilton.. 161

If Only They Could Talk by Eva Leppard............................... 181

This is the Dawning (Part V) by Helena McAuley................. 191

FOREWORD

Sasha Hanton

Strong, grounded and bull-headed are just a few terms used to describe the second sign of the zodiac. Represented by a bull is Taurus, the fixed earth sign ruled over by the ever-lovely planet of Venus.

The mythology surrounding Taurus comes from the Greek myth of Europa. When the god, Zeus, was enraptured by the beauty of King Agenor of Tyre's daughter he disguised himself as a handsome white bull. One day whilst Europa was walking near the water, she spotted this magnificent bull grazing amongst her father's herd. As she approached the beast knelt in front of her as if to permit her to ride it, Europa climbed upon its back and when she was seated it leapt to its feet and charged off into the sea.

The bull eventually stopped on the shores of Crete and Zeus revealed his true form before seducing Europa. Though this is the most famous myth linked to Taurus there are other myths that feature bulls and carry significance to Taurus, which can be found in Mesopotamian, Egyptian and other mythologies. Even within Greek mythology there is another story with ties to the constellation, that of Zeus' lover Io who he transformed into a heifer to disguise from Hera, and other myths featuring bulls.

As with each member of the zodiac Taurus has a specific connection to a card from the Major Arcana of the Tarot, in Taurus' case that is the Hierophant. With two initiates kneeling before him the Hierophant sits between two pillars wearing a triple crown and holding a sceptre with the triple cross, at his feet are the crossed keys of the hidden doctrine. It may be interpreted as a religious card but at its root it is a card of conformity, bowing to social norms, and in the reverse it can be about gullibility, unconventional thinking, and being outside the norm. Whilst symbolically you might not see the connection between this card and Taurus it is there, the pillars behind the Hierophant represent stability and the two initiates before him show that he brings people together. Taurus is often lauded as the most dependable sign of the zodiac; they are loyal and reliable forces of stability in the lives of their friends.

Overseen by the planet Venus—who also rules over Libra—Taureans are often loving and friendly. Named after the Roman Goddess of love and beauty, Venus imbues its subjects with a love for all the best things and keen senses to enjoy them with.

If you were born between April 20th and May 20th then there's no doubt you're a Taurus. Those with Taurus as their Sun sign tend to be gentle, compassionate, and easy to get along with although at times they can be more stubborn than a bull.

This stalwart sign may seem easy to get a read on but as you peer into this labyrinth of stories you're sure to find hidden depths to Taurus.

About the Author:

Sasha Hanton grew up in the tropics of Darwin, Northern Territory. From a young age, she devoured books and iced coffee, both of which she continues to intake on an almost daily basis. Now living on beautiful Bribie Island in Queensland, her time is split between writing and spoiling her puppy Miley.

Sasha, who has a Bachelor of Journalism from Bond University, has dabbled in the journalistic profession but finds fiction far more fascinating. Her first published work The Short Story Press Collection *draws on her love for a diverse range of genres and passion for short stories. Coming from a multicultural background (Eurasian) she aspires to make her writing inclusive for people from all walks of life and to bring a unique blend of eastern and western culture to her writing.*

Throughout her life, she has been a lover of history and mythology, and at any time will find some way to worm one or the other into her storytelling. When she's not writing or reading she can be found walking her dog and volunteering. You can keep up with her writing over on www.theshortstorypress.wordpress.com

THE BULL OF HEAVEN

Alannah K. Pearson

I woke to the trill of a blackbird. Weak sunlight struggled to push through dense cloud cover and the morning air was crisp. My dog lifted his head from the bed, opening a bleary eye to glare reproachfully toward the window. Lance was a rescue dog, the mystery of his canine parentage reflected in his disproportionately long ears and wiry brindle coat. The blackbird called again, and Lance sighed, jumped from the bed and trotted purposefully toward the back door. My yard was mostly wild and overgrown except for a small paved courtyard where Lance and the blackbird had an ongoing war over territory. Sighing with resignation, I climbed from the warm bed covers.

My bare feet scuffed across the chill slate tiles of the kitchen. Quickly I opened the sliding glass door, letting Lance into the yard before I turned away from the cold morning air, and flicked the switch of the coffee machine. While waiting for the coffee to brew, I twisted my long blond hair into a loose bun. I halted, catching sight of my reflection in the window glass. I barely recognised the thinner woman dressed in yesterday's wrinkled clothing. I thought for a moment of how my husband had never understood my obsession to detail, my compulsion for orderliness. He would not recognise you either, I thought, the memory of his death hit me again like a blow. Turning away from my reflection and painful memories, I focused on my tasks for the day.

I poured a cup of coffee, inhaling the familiar inviting aroma. I decided I would try taming part of the overgrown garden, a section extending beyond the confines of the small courtyard. I had recently moved to this small rural Australian village, several hundred kilometres from the nearest major city. This town was old, originally constructed at a crossroad of two intersecting thoroughfares between the main capital cities. But with the passage of time, new roads bypassed this once-vital artery and now the hamlet was almost empty, nature had already reclaimed what humans had constructed. In the decades this house had stood empty, the garden seemed somehow wilder than the surrounding forests, the vines easily consuming garden walls and veranda alike. If I were to make some semblance of a new life in this place, I needed to tame the garden.

I finished my coffee and rolled up my sleeves, ignoring the pulse of guilt that I had slept in yesterday's clothes. None of that matters, I told myself. None of it matters when he is dead. Gritting my teeth, I strode into the courtyard, sunlight beginning to pierce the morning fog and started clearing the ground in the garden where I would construct a new stone wall. Sitting on my heels, I manoeuvred the hand-trowel, mechanically scraping away detritus from the long-abandoned garden beds. Beside me, a pile of broken roofing tiles, fragments of charred timber and broken terracotta pots grew. Behind me, Lance bounded around the yard while I wiped the back of my dirt-smeared hand across my forehead. Midday was approaching and already the warmth of the day seemed to leach back into the cold earth. Winter clouds scudded across the brilliant blue sky and a breeze rattled bare branches like sabres.

Shivering, I scraped away another section of dark soil, revealing a sand-stained shard of pottery. The incongruous light-coloured clay fragment drew my attention, and I peered closer at the shard, amazed at how none of the surrounding moist soil clung to the pottery fragment nor how any was ingrained in the uneven texture of the clay surface. I smoothed a finger across the pottery, revealing some carved inscriptions. The palm-sized piece fitted neatly in my hand and was smooth on the sides as though time had caressed the sharpness from the edges.

I stood up; trowel forgotten beside the garden bed. Walking carefully to the small garden table, I cradled the pottery fragment in my hands. Squinting at the inscriptions, I realised they appeared deliberate, markings covering every available surface of the pottery piece. It was not a pattern, or if it was, I did not recognise it. I leaned back on the wrought iron chair, eyes closed, face tilted up to the midday sky. An inexplicable knowledge coalesced that this pottery was old, and, equally strange, the certainty that if I lifted the pottery closer, I would hear the hissing of desert winds.

A voice whispered close behind me. "Release the bull of heaven."

I stared at the inscription, gaze unfocused and frowned. I shook my head, half-twisting to stare at the empty space behind my left shoulder. Did I imagine a voice? Had it been real? I shivered at the implications of hallucinating but more fearful still was the unwanted intrusion into my usually orderly mind. Lance whined beside me, breaking the fugue of strangeness that engulfed me. I shook my head then stood so abruptly I nearly knocked the chair to the paving stones. Without hesitation, I moved inside the house, still holding the odd clay fragment in my hands. Although I walked purposefully, I could not ignore the uncomfortable awareness of a presence behind me.

Once in the kitchen, I placed the pottery fragment on the counter-top, the clink of the clay against the hard surface seemed to echo in the quiet house. My hand trembled as I reached for my phone. There was something I could not explain about the pottery, the inscriptions and the texture of the clay itself that jarred against reality. After uploading the photo I had taken, I searched for similar images online. Although I wanted to justify my instinct that this was some ancient and unusual pottery fragment, I equally wanted the comforting confirmation that my thoughts were ludicrous. Surely, I was just being over-imaginative?

Less than a few brief seconds later, I had the answers I sought. I stared at the screen, the rows of many small images, each showing a pottery piece similar to the one I had found. I scrolled through the images with growing consternation. If I had hoped for clarification and some closure, this did not achieve it. Many of the images contained brief descriptions, with the same word repeated throughout. The pottery pieces were known as cuneiform tablets and all were related to museum collections. What on earth was cuneiform? I frowned, reaching across the counter for my laptop. I needed to expand my search and find out what cuneiform was, whether it was as ancient as my instinct warned me it was. Most of all, I wanted to understand why a cuneiform tablet had been buried in my garden.

The answers provided by an online search seemed improbable. Every article explained that cuneiform script was an ancient proto-writing system that had developed in the Near East over six-thousand years ago. My frown deepened as I considered the implications. How did cuneiform tablets become buried in my garden? Australia was a long way from the ancient empires of Iraq. Was the tablet in my yard evidence from some illegal trading or forgery attempts? I shook my head slowly at my rational attempts to explain an impossible event.

I continued to read, realisation dawning on how unlikely my discovery had been. Cuneiform was the common writing system between the ancient kingdoms of Sumeria, Babylon, Assyria and Persia. Again, I felt a keen awareness of a presence behind me. Half-turning from the kitchen counter, I was almost expecting someone to be standing a foot behind me. There was no one. I shivered, returning my attention to the search results. It's an impossibility, I reminded myself. You've never studied ancient texts; you've never even travelled to Iraq. Cuneiform tablets simply don't just appear from thin air. This is madness.

Although it was ridiculous to think the pottery I had found was a genuine cuneiform tablet, I continued to learn the fascinating history of these small palm-sized tablets made by ancient cultures several millennia ago and half a world away.

Daylight faded outside and as afternoon stretched into twilight, I continued to read. Even as I considered quitting this strange obsession to learn more, my gaze fell on the title of a poem and it flared in my consciousness as though some brilliant beacon. The Epic of Gilgamesh; an ancient poem detailing the struggle between a Sumerian king and the powerful gods. The awareness behind me grew suddenly stronger, transforming from a presence to a prickling on my skin, as though long fingers danced across my back. I slapped at my shoulder, certain it was just a spider or another insect. My hands found no insect, but the prickling worsened, now feeling as if a chill breath touched the back of my neck. I wanted to move, to flee, but instead I glanced warily behind me, certain someone leaned close to me, almost touching my left shoulder. Again, there was no one.

"Get a grip," I muttered, trying to enforce calmness and rationality.

I returned my attention to the computer screen. The Epic of Gilgamesh was recorded in cuneiform, inscribed on similar palm-sized clay tablets as the one I had found. It told the deeds of the heroic Sumerian king Gilgamesh and how he overcame philosophical dilemmas during his battles against the ancient gods. I paused, suddenly unsure what had seemed so important to me about The Epic of Gilgamesh. I shook my head slightly and refocused on the page. One phrase seemed to illuminate amid the surrounding lines of text. The Bull of Heaven. Perspiration broke out across my skin and my heartbeat quickened. I had heard those words whispered to me in the garden. I had not imagined the hissing voice and now that same phrase was written down here. What was the Bull of Heaven? Whatever was happening to me it didn't seem like some mental breakdown or an odd delusion. This was more than that, a coincidence on a higher level I could not deny. I inhaled slowly and opened the link to another document, determined to learn whatever I could about the Bull of Heaven.

According to the myth, Gilgamesh angers the goddess Ishtar who sends the destructive Bull of Heaven to extract her vengeance. Gilgamesh, however, slays the mythical bull and dismembers it, casting the hindquarters into the sky to form the constellation synonymous with Taurus.

A strong but inexplicable fear and precognition shivered through me. I stopped reading, titling my head and straining my hearing. I thought I had heard a faint chuckle. Now there was only the silence of the evening and the distant ticking of a clock. I shrugged, returning my attention to the screen.

Before long, I discovered another account of the Gilgamesh story, a much older form where Ishtar had another, more ancient name: Inanna. The goddess Inanna was the daughter of the sun and moon deities and in vengeance for an unknown offence, Inanna sent the Bull of Heaven against Gilgamesh. In this poem, the Bull of Heaven was more than a mythic beast to be slain by a heroic king. Inanna had a much darker nature, the goddess of bounty was also the goddess of famine and when she unleashed the Bull of Heaven upon the world, it delivered Inanna's vengeance in famine, fire and destruction. Fortunately, Gilgamesh still slays the Bull of Heaven, and prevents the destruction Inanna had sought.

I finished reading, a cold fear settling over me as I stared at several depictions of the Bull of Heaven, the muscular form carved into stone on temple walls, inscribed into gold and silver, shaped into tiny statues and icons. In every representation, the bull was a formidable beast with horns lowered to charge, one hoof raised in challenge.

After dinner, I walked outside into the shadowed garden, following the meandering step-stone path. I halted and exhaled, my breath an icy cloud in the night. I tilted my face upward, staring at the bare winter branches silhouetted against the night sky. I searched the starry dome, seeking the constellation of Taurus, following the path of the Milky Way, noticing the brighter points of significant stars which were, nonetheless, still nameless and unfamiliar to me. The night sky was as peaceful as always and that familiar sensation seemed to absorb the dislocation threatening to engulf me. I smiled in the darkness, fascinated by the shimmer of stardust along the Milky Way and I felt complete again as I had not been since my husband's death.

When the cold became too much for even the most determined stargazer, I hurried back toward the house, hands stuffed into the pockets of my old dressing gown. I paused at the glass door, smiling back at the night and reached for the door handle. Perhaps it was because I wasn't paying attention, but my fingers slipped on the handle, falling instead to the empty earth of the window-box beside the door. The window-box was devoid of plants this early in winter and yet my fingertips touched textured surface that was not soil. I held myself still, heart pounding as I moved my fingers along the now-familiar clay surface, exploring the inscriptions that covered the uneven shape of the clay tablet.

"Bring forth Inanna's vengeance, let the world be reborn," a voice hissed behind me, tone like shifting sand against stone.

I shivered violently, fear rising and drenching me in sudden perspiration. I fled inside, my traitorous fingers grasping the clay-tablet in a reaction I could not explain.

Once inside, I pushed my back to the kitchen counter, breathing quickly, staring in surprise at the tablet I held. Incomprehension consumed me as I stared from the cuneiform tablet in my hands to the one on the counter top. Wordless sobs tore from me and I slowly sunk to the kitchen floor. I cradled my head in my hands, trying to stifle the sounds breaking unbidden from my throat. Lance whined uncertainly from the doorway and approached, tail wagging as he climbed into my lap. The reality of the madness engulfing me seemed stark and I could no longer hide from it.

I woke in the early hours, slumped awkwardly on the kitchen floor. Morning was just beginning to blush across the eastern horizon, barely a smudge against the darkness of night. Lance was still curled in my lap, but I was bitterly cold. I uncurled my cramped limbs, urging Lance to get up so I could climb stiffly to my feet. I stole a quick glance at the two cuneiform tablets on the kitchen countertop before hastening toward the bedroom, hoping for the oblivion of sleep.

I was chilled and frightened as I stepped into my bedroom, filled with the horrible sensation that someone followed behind me. I halted near my bed, staring at the empty expanse, the space my husband used to occupy that would be forever vacant. I shivered in the cold predawn air and took a desperate step toward the bed.

My bare toes touched an object, half-hidden beneath the overhang of my bed covers. I sucked in a breath with a hiss. I wanted to recoil, to flee. This could not be another clay tablet. My world seemed to spin around me, the future balanced precariously on my next action. I slid my foot back and saw the now-familiar cuneiform script on the surface of the pottery. I stared in disbelief and felt the future shift toward a decisive moment. The constant presence behind me coalesced.

"With Inanna's vengeance slaked, all will grow anew from ashes and bones," the awful voice whispered, breath tickling my ear.

"Go away," I shouted, slapping ridiculously at my ears as if that could somehow silence the voice.

"You don't truly want me to leave," the voice mocked.

"What are you?" I demanded, aware it lingered behind me and half-expecting if I turned around, it would be visible in the doorway.

"I have many names," it hissed. "We have been known as jinn or demons, but we are neither."

"What do you want then?" I pleaded.

"What you desire most of all," the thing crooned.

My anguish was a sound that seemed to shatter the room, slivers of myself spinning in every direction, reflecting back images of my face contorted with terror, fingers raking at my cheeks.

I ran into the sunroom, knees finally buckling, dropping to the floor. Lance skidded to a halt beside me, hackles raised as he stared at the empty space near the window. I looked at the large window that covered the northern side of the room but could discern nothing but my own reflection. I stared at my pale face smeared with tears and gave a sharp cry of frustration, scrubbing roughly at my cheeks, trying to enforce some composure. The awful panic that had taken hold seemed to subside and I sat back on my heels, looking out the northern window as dawn light broke through the morning clouds. I sensed through some precognitive awareness that this was the last dawn I would ever see. The dense cloud mass was already spreading like a blight across the sky, and soon not even the bright morning sunlight would stop it. Alongside that awful realisation came a sense of claustrophobia as though the air itself pressed upon me, as if it were a tangible, heavy weight.

"Release the bull of heaven." The jinn urged me again.

"Shut up!" I shouted into the silence.

The jinn only laughed, a deep horrible sound that reverberated through the room and sent tremors shuddering through me. I cried nonsensical objections, promised impossible threats, but that taunting voice continued to ripple with laughter. When finally my terror peaked, I scooted backward across the floor, slamming my right shoulder hard into the window ledge. I cried out in pain, echoed by a sharp clatter from behind me that sent another wave of uncontrollable trembling through my body. I turned my head slowly, expecting to see the jinn from the periphery of my vision. There was nothing there, like all the times before. *This is a hallucination. There will never be anything there*, I reminded myself. I slumped forward in exhaustion, relief rolling through me as I bent my head to my knees. That's when I noticed the fourth cuneiform tablet. It must have fallen when I hit the window ledge. I watched as though from outside myself as my fingers reached for the clay fragment. I lifted it, turning it over in my hand, marvelling at the unnatural heaviness of the small tablet.

"With Inanna's cry, the bull will stamp the earth to dust and vengeance be claimed in her name," the jinn pronounced with dreadful certainty.

Time passed, or perhaps it no longer existed. I sat in the shadows of the sunroom, cuneiform tablet gripped in my hands as a storm descended on the afternoon, the last of the sunlight cutting thin slivers through the black clouds. The room was suffocating, the sense of anticipation seeming to crush the oxygen from the air itself. I struggled to breathe, fought to master my panic that an unavoidable calamity approached. The rooms seemed too small, the temperature was stifling and outside, the sky was too dark. The storm had not broken but seemed to wait, tense and patient, swollen with unleashed rage. The jinn was a menacing presence filling my small house, taunts and cries flushed with exultation.

"Inanna?" I called, uncertain but pleading into the growing shadow of the storm.

The jinn suddenly halted its rapturous cries and listened, silence falling heavy around me.

"Inanna?" I called firmly, heart beating loudly as I lifted my face to the gloom outside my window. "Inanna!" I shouted, calling on the name of the goddess again, this time an invocation.

"Do you know who you seek, mortal child?" the jinn asked in a hushed whisper.

"Please stop this," I begged, burying my face in my hand, leaning heavily against the window frame.

"Ah," the jinn cooed. "Only Inanna can grant you that release you seek."

"Tell me how," I sobbed, clutching at my hair as though pulling it from my scalp would stop this madness.

Across the room, Lance growled and stood, legs apart with short hackles raised, but did not approach, just stared at the emptiness behind me. Again, I desperately wanted to twist away. I felt the icy prickle of fingertips brush on my cheek and I might have been frozen beneath that touch.

"Only you hold the power to grant Inanna's wish," the jinn said. "In granting her wish, your desire will be returned in kind."

"How?" I sobbed again, wanting to move away from the horrible being that seemed to lurk behind me. I forced myself to hold firm, to ignore the frigid breath on the back of my neck that burned like fire. I barely repressed a shudder as, around me, the pressure of the storm increased and with it, a throbbing pain blossomed in my skull.

"You know what to do," the jinn said.

My eyes focused on the cuneiform tablet beside my foot. I did not let myself think but focused my attention on the uneven edges of the pottery shard. Suddenly, I could see where it had been broken from a whole, where the other fragments had once fitted around it.

"Does it make a poem?" I asked, picking up the tablet. "Does it tell a story like Gilgamesh?"

The jinn howled in rage; the noise reverberated through the house like the screeching against stone. I clutched at my ears, trying to lessen the noise but it seemed to tear the air to shreds around it.

"Not a story of destruction like Gilgamesh," the jinn snarled.

"But it tells a story?" I asked, dizziness engulfing me as my vision spun.

"Yes," the jinn replied. "The false hero Gilgamesh is long buried beneath the sands of time, but these lands have never known the stamp of hoof. It is Inanna's greatest wish that such a power remind them of their faith."

I tried to consider the jinn's words but the pain inside my skull climbed to a crescendo, the throbbing of my eardrums nearly deafening but I still heard the rasping voice of the jinn behind me.

"Work quickly, mortal child," it advised.

I moved as swiftly as I could, my legs trembling as I gripped the clay tablet, blood dripping from my nostrils. I ran into the kitchen, quickly rearranging the clay fragments, guided by an unfathomable intuition. When I was finished, I stared at the arranged fragments, the centre still a dark and yawning void. Hastily, I wiped away more droplets of blood falling onto the counter-top, carefully manoeuvring the final piece of pottery into place. The final fragment was the most recent, the one that had fallen from the window-ledge in the sunroom. I stared at it, noticing that, unlike the other tablets, this one contained no cuneiform inscriptions but depicted the Bull of Heaven—horns lowered, muscular body tensed, and one hoof raised to crush an enemy beneath it.

I did not allow myself time to think. I ignored the pain in my fingers as the sharp edges of the clay sliced my skin. I moved with near reverence, carefully lowering the final fragment into place, the uneven margins smoothing away to reveal the tablet, whole and complete as though it had never been broken.

The pressure in the atmosphere dropped, the storm grew quiet and silence descended. I could hear nothing since the jinn had screamed at me. Now, in confusion, I turned to survey the windows of the sunroom. I looked down in bewilderment at the stain across my shirt, the blood still trickling from my nose. I lifted my eyes again to the windows and with a quickening of my heart, I walked towards them.

Outside, the massive storm clouds now swarmed across the sky, turning in a slow spiral, edged with flame.

"What have I done?" I whispered.

"What you desired," the jinn chuckled with apparent glee.

"Just tell me what I did!" I shouted.

The silence crackled, paused, before a roar of thunder split the sky. The wind burst into a gale, hurling debris and leaves across my garden, increasing in strength that shook the large windows of the sunroom. Cautiously, I stepped back from the glass panes, expecting them to shatter from the onslaught. Lance whined piteously from my bedroom doorway; ears flat as he glared toward me. No, I realised. Not at me but behind me.

"Inanna granted you the release you sought," the jinn explained. "And in kind, you released the Bull of Heaven."

"But what does that mean?" I roared against the tempest outside.

"Didn't you understand the summoning?" the jinn mocked. "The bull will bring these lands into subservience."

I remembered the poem from the cuneiform tablets, and all the jinn had quoted to me.

"Bring forth Inanna's vengeance and let the world be reborn. For only when Inanna's vengeance is slaked, will all grow anew from ashes and bones. With Inanna's cry, the bull will stamp the earth to dust and vengeance be claimed in her name. Release the bull of heaven."

"Exactly," the jinn said jovially. "The foolish mortals of these lands sought to challenge the might of the gods. Millennia may have passed, child, but this is the briefest of moments to the gods. Inanna now takes her vengeance for the defiance of mortal men."

I blinked in dumb confusion. "Inanna is punishing us now for the actions of Gilgamesh?" I asked. "Those actions committed thousands of years ago?"

"Yes," the jinn snapped with irritation. "Inanna does not discriminate between her children. You may think you acted as one, but his punishment befalls you all."

"How did I do this?" I asked, gesturing to the flame touched sky, ash now falling from the clouds like rain.

"How else?" the jinn asked. "If Gilgamesh was only one man who committed an injustice, why would it matter if one mortal restores the balance and delivers justice?"

"Justice?" I croaked, staring in horror at the fiery sky outside.

"To gods like Inanna, this is justice," the jinn explained. "It should not bother you, mortal. For now, you are free."

I stared in bitter wonder at the destruction I had unleashed. "Free from what?"

"From me," the jinn chuckled.

I turned then, noticing a sudden spray of sparks behind me. Dark tendrils of smoke spiralled upward, evaporating almost as quickly as the half-visible form of the grinning jinn, simply vanished. I felt the sudden departure of the jinn as though oxygen had been pulled from the air. I lurched forward, clutching the window frame for support. I pressed my face to the glass, unable to stand as my legs weakened. I leaned on the window frame for support, forcing myself to witness Inanna's merciless vengeance borne from my own actions.

I stood mute; a soundless scream caught in my throat as dark clouds edged with lightning coalesced into the massive form of a bull. I tasted bile as the Bull of Heaven lowered wicked horns crafted from lightning. The beast stamped a hoof, molten rain showering down on the earth below, birthing wildfires and flushing the sky an angry red. Tears left ashen tracks down my face as the Bull of Heaven moved across the sky and, where it briefly touched the earth, decimation lay in its wake. After moments that could have been eons, the Bull of Heaven raised its massive head and bellowed a challenge like thunder, hoof stamping and sending more fiery tornadoes across the barren earth below. A hollow silence echoed from the land around me and with a toss of its muscular head, I watched as Inanna's vengeance was finally slaked and the bull retreated.

For a long time I stood there, clutching the window frame of my small house, the landscape surrounding me now a wasteland of burnt forest and charred rock. Clouds of black smoke blew across the window, hiding the barren lands beyond. I did not think anyone could have survived the devastation I had unwittingly unleashed, but I had to save anyone I could. I walked unsteadily to my door and with one glance knew Inanna's vengeance for the destruction it was, for wherever the Bull of Heaven had stood, only ash and embers remained.

About the Author:

Alannah K. Pearson is a speculative fiction author, her writing combining archaeology and ancient history, inspired by global legends and mythologies with strong fable qualities, especially those strongly influenced by the natural environment.

Alannah's debut adult Fantasy novel, Bone Arrow, *inspired by Amerindian fables and legends is currently available as an ebook. Alannah is currently completing an adult fantasy novel, inspired by Norse mythology and legends. In 2020, two short stories will feature in anthologies, a dystopian fantasy inspired by ancient Mesopotamian mythology in* Taurus: The Zodiac Series *published by Deadset Press and a fantasy inspired by environmental folklore and legends in* Unnatural Order *to be published by Canberra Speculative Fiction Group.*

Alannah K. Pearson lives in Canberra, Australia. You can follow her updates from her website www.alannahkpearson.com and on social media @AlannahKPearson.

PLEIADES

Jenny Blackford

Between the
nearby streetlights
and Taurus' red bullseye,
the sisters dance
so close, so tight

that every time
you try to count,
you get to six
and a half
or five
and two-thirds,
never quite to

seven.

Some say
the seventh sister
is the loveliest.

Some say

that she's gone bush.

Some say

they've danced with her

high in the blue.

Clouds of shy stars

drift in their eyes.

About the Author:

Jenny is an award-winning Australian writer and poet. Her poems and stories have appeared in Asimov's Science Fiction, Cosmos, Westerly, Strange Horizons *and many more Australian and international journals and anthologies.*

Legendary feminist writer Pamela Sargent called her novella set in ancient Greece, The Priestess and the Slave, *"elegant". She won two prizes in the Sisters in Crime Australia Scarlet Stiletto awards 2016 for a murder mystery set in classical Delphi, with water nymphs. Eagle Books published her spidery, ghostly middle-grade novel* The Girl in the Mirror *in October 2019. Pitt Street Poetry published* The Duties of a Cat *in 2013,* The Loyalty of Chickens *in 2017, and her third poetry collection,* The Alpaca Cantos, *in April 2020.*

Website www.jennyblackford.com
Twitter @dutiesofacat
Facebook https://www.facebook.com/jennyblackford

THE BODY IN THE WALL

Stephen Herczeg

"Gidday folks and welcome back," said Stewie Gould, the well-built ex-chippy and compere of the home renovation show *Flat out Renos*, as he stared down the camera lens.

A four-story building towered above him. The front entrance needed some tender loving care, with the brass doors hanging by a single hinge and the two bull head statues on either side, dirty from decades of exhaust fumes and smoke. Stewie stood on the wide fenced off pathway that led to the doors. The path acted almost like a bridge above the moat formed by the two basement courtyards that ran around the entire building. To one side a stone staircase led into the courtyard, and the entire area was protected all around by a tall wrought iron fence that stopped any unwary pedestrians from falling the three metres to the broken stone paving below.

"Two weeks ago, our four couples moved into the derelict remains of Thurley Towers. A once grand building from the turn of last century, it's been out of use for decades." Stewie turned towards the building. "And it shows. Just the place for a good old fashioned reno."

He winked at the camera and continued on. "Our couples have finished off their master bedrooms and en suites, which is a good way to start the competition, and now we don't have to put them up at an expensive hotel every night. This week they are working on their living rooms. Up in the penthouse, the 'Power Couple' Elijah and Petra are doing everything they can to impress the judges with lux on lux. 'Young Parents' Brad and Shelley on level two have chosen a subtler approach, just like 'ex-Rugby star' Ivan and his 'wag' Mischa at the ground level. Meanwhile, down in the dungeon—sorry basement— our 'Professional Tradies' Chris and Jenna have decided that the area is just not big enough."

Stewie paused for a moment to allow for a cutaway then asked, "was that okay?"

Doug, the Director, nodded.

Stewie smiled and wiped his brow. "Geez, that was a long mono and it's stinking hot," he said. "Is it beer o'clock yet?"

Down in the basement apartment, Andy trained the camera on Chris and Jenna as they argued, again, over details on the house plans that were spread out before them.

Chris flipped the plan over, revealing a blueprint and pointed to a vacant part of the room. He looked over his shoulder at a small outcrop of plastered brick that jutted out from the main stone wall. "I'm telling you, it's not on the originals. The wall was flat all the way. This was added later."

Chris walked across to the strange addition and knocked. A hollow echo came from within. He stepped up to the main wall and knocked again. It was as solid as the rock used to build it.

"See?" he said. "It's hollow. Therefore, not part of the main wall." Chris looked around all the corners of the protruding part of the wall and knocked a few more times. He turned back to Jenna and smiled, then stepped across to his tools and picked up a sledgehammer.

Jenna gasped in shock. "You can't be serious," she said. "We'd have to check with the builder before doing something like this."

"Ah, bugger him. It's not a supporting wall. It's hollow. It's an afterthought. If we get rid of it, we get another couple of square metres and a nice long flat wall." He approached the wall and tapped the base with the head of the sledge a couple of times, each harder than the last.

Suddenly, an entire sheet of plaster detached and crashed to the floor, sending Chris running. Dust flew up in a cloud, obscuring the wall for a moment and enveloping the two of them. Chris snatched the plastic safety goggles from his face and rubbed his eyes to clear the plaster dust. "Stupid cheap bastards, these things are useless," he said.

Jenna nodded, removing her own goggles and wiping at her eyes.

Andy, his own eyes protected by the camera's viewfinder, kept focus on the wall. As the dust settled a hidden patch of stonework showed itself. His eyes widened at the sight. "Guys, you might want to check this out."

Jenna saw it first. "Oh, my God," she said, grabbing for her phone to take a photo.

"What?" said Chris still rubbing at his eyes. He blinked a few times and stared towards the wall. As his eyes cleared, he finally saw it. "Holy crap," he said, stepping towards the image on the wall.

Carved into the brickwork was a large bull's head, overlaid with an inverted pentagram nestled inside a circle. Several words in an archaic script were written along the edges of the circle.

Jenna's flash went off several times. She stared at the photos on her phone. "What do you think it is?" she asked.

"No idea. Just some graffiti that the previous owners covered up?" Chris said.

Jenna stepped up to the wall and ran a finger along the carved lines. "But it's carved, not painted. This had meaning to someone. Carving it meant they wanted it to remain in place for years."

"Fine. It won't have any meaning soon." He hefted the sledge and tapped it against the bottom rows of bricks.

A hollow noise rang out through the room.

He brought the sledge back and said, "Okay then."

The sledgehammer slammed into the bricks, shattered the mortar and sent a couple of bricks into the void beyond. A cloud of putrid air rushed out of the gap and enveloped Jenna.

Outside on the street, Stewie faced the camera and began another monologue. "While Ivan struggles to complete the sheeting in their ground floor lounge, Mischa wanders around the local shopping mall searching for that vital statement piece that the judges will just love. Shelley has gone with Mischa to—"

"Cut," said Doug.

Stewie looked at him confused. "What was wrong with that?"

Doug pointed over his shoulder and walked forwards. He peered through the tall wrought iron railing into the basement courtyard beyond. Kneeling amongst the debris, Jenna threw up the entire contents of her stomach in great wracking heaves.

"You okay Jenna?" called Stewie. He and Doug quickly moved to the nearby stairs and descended into the courtyard.

Just as Doug reached Jenna, Chris appeared at the doorway with the sledgehammer resting on his shoulder. A beaming smile belied the fact his wife was vomiting at his feet. "You guys need to see this," he said.

As soon as Doug and Stewie followed Chris into the room the cloying smell of putrescence hit them. They both coughed and gagged.

Chris laughed, "Horrible ain't it? I haven't smelt anything that bad since I hit a week-old roo and it splattered through the open window of my truck." He walked over to the fake wall and tapped it with the sledge. Still grinning he said, "Check this out."

With tears streaming from their eyes, Stewie and Doug stepped over to look through the hole Chris had made.

It was too small to be a room. It was more a bricked-up cupboard. Lying curled in an untidy heap on the floor was a desiccated corpse. The flesh was long dissolved, leaving the paper-thin skin clinging desperately to the bones beneath. The clothes had disintegrated into rags along with the flesh. A single hand stretched out towards the men as they stared into the hollow.

"Gross," said a voice behind them. They all turned to see Ayesha, the Producer, standing in the doorway. She was looking at the discarded pool of vomit outside. Jenna was nowhere in sight.

"Think that's bad, you should see this," said Chris.

Doug stood by and watched the two paramedics grunting and groaning as they pulled the body out of the hollow. With every movement it creaked, groaned and snapped as its ancient tendons, ligaments and bones ground against each other. As they stepped backwards the head lolled to one side at an impossible angle and threatened to break off.

Chris stepped in and grabbed the back of the head before it could come away. He grimaced at the spidery touch of the corpse's hair but kept hold until it was loaded onto the gurney. "This dude is nasty as." He grimaced, wiping his hands on his shorts to remove the brick dust and any remains from the corpse.

"How do you know it's a dude?" asked Elijah. The other couples had come downstairs as the news spread throughout the complex. All the contestants and crew crowded into the room as the paramedics and police worked. Various expressions of disgust and fascination crossed their faces as they watched the goings on.

"His clothes," said Chris. "That was a suit jacket and a bow tie. I don't reckon many sheilas would have worn those in the past."

Doug stood near the gurney and leaned in to one of the paramedics. "How long do you think it's been in there?"

The paramedic held up the corpse's hand then looked back at the hollow. "A damn long time. There's no flesh or fat left. Skin is as tough as leather. Dunno really. Maybe a few decades? Hundred years? Coroner will figure it out." He turned back to the corpse's hand and continued, "This is disturbing though."

"What is?"

The paramedic showed the ends of the fingers, which were devoid of skin, the bones poking through. "His fingers. There's no skin on the end. He must have scraped them bloody. That means he was bricked up alive in there."

"Oh, God," said Doug.

The paramedics secured the corpse to the gurney and wheeled it out to the ambulance.

Doug stood looking at the hollow.

Ayesha walked up next to him and stared as well. "I told you this was a bad idea," she said. Her phone made clicking noises as she fired off a couple of photos of the design.

"It can't be him. He disappeared over a hundred years ago. Went to England they said," Doug said.

"Yeah. And I'm gonna be the next Prime Minister," Ayesha said then turned and left the room.

A policeman walked over. Doug remembered he'd introduced himself as Constable Matt Cooper. He pointed at the hollow. "We're pretty much done here, but we're gonna need this room sealed off for a few days until we do a full examination of that."

Doug nodded, "No problems. We'll get the couple to work on another room."

"Yeah, I don't care about that, just don't disturb this room okay?" Cooper turned and saw his partner taking a selfie with Stewie Gould. "Jones what are you doing?" he asked.

The other policeman smiled widely. "Mate, this is Stewie Gould, he's a dead set legend." Jones shook Stewie's hand before the presenter walked away.

The other couples began to disperse. The excitement was over, and they had work to do.

Petra followed. There was a lot to do in the penthouse and this little interruption would cause a delay.

I wonder if there's anything like this upstairs. We could always use more room.

Petra took one last look at the hollow in the wall. Her eyes saw a glint of gold and opened wider in surprise. She stopped and waited for the rest to leave before venturing back to the opening. She hunkered down and reached for the shiny object.

Petra pulled at it and drew a light golden chain from the pile of dust and debris. Finally, it was followed by a golden pendant. She brushed off the dust and held it up. It was a round medallion with a black ebony insert. Inlaid into the ebony, in pure gold, was the head of a bull. The eyes on the bull sparkled a brilliant white like diamonds.

Petra smiled.

This must be worth a fortune.

She quickly wound the chain around the medallion and stuffed it into her pocket, standing up just as Elijah poked his head into the room.

"Hey, you coming? We've still got a lot of painting to do," he said.

Doug's phone lit up as an unknown number rang through at 6:30 the next morning. Thinking it was one of the contestants using a different phone, he answered. "Yeah, what the hell?" he said.

"Mr. Wade?" said a stern voice on the other end.

"Yes?"

"This is Constable Matt Cooper. We met yesterday."

Recognition dawned. "Oh, yeah, sorry didn't recognise the voice. What's up?"

"You need to get to the site now," Cooper said.

Doug's heart sank as soon as he stepped into the basement apartment. Constable Cooper's face was a mask of anger, as he stared daggers at the director.

"I told you to seal this area off," Cooper said.

Confused, Doug's eyes fell on the piles of bricks and plaster that littered the floor. Then he realised, the entire internal structure of the little hollow had been torn down since the day before. The dust and debris that covered the area inside the hollow had been dug through and strewn about the room. Chris, a wide grin on his face, Jenna and Ayesha stood nearby gaping at the damage.

Doug started to answer but Cooper cut him off.

"This is unacceptable. The whole crime scene has been disturbed. If any evidence has been lost, I'll put the blame solely on you," he said poking Doug in the chest.

Doug turned towards Chris and Jenna. Both shrugged.

"We called them when we found it like this. We were working on the kitchen all yesterday arvo and were in bed until six this morning," Chris said.

Mischa walked in, her hair out of place and a groggy look on her face. She directed her question at Jenna. "What were you two doing down here last night? It was bang, crash and scrape all damn night," she said then gazed at the damage. "Hang on, I thought you weren't allowed in here?" she asked.

"They weren't," said Cooper before storming off followed by his partner.

Chris smiled and spoke up, "It wasn't us and I don't care who it was because it's saved us a bunch of time."

"What the hell happened here?"

Elijah's voice floated into the penthouse bedroom, shocking Petra out of a deep sleep. She sat up and felt the golden amulet knock against her chest. She placed a hand on it and smiled.

Should be worth a mint when we get out of here.

She dressed and wandered out to see what had upset her short-tempered husband this time.

Elijah was running his fingers along several deep scratches in the freshly painted wall of their living area.

"Holy crap," she said.

"Crap is right. I'm going to give someone crap," he spat and stormed out of the room.

Petra watched him go then removed the necklace. She stared at it and smiled again. "I'll just lock you up to keep you safe during the day," she said.

Elijah stormed into the dining room to find the other couples seated around the tables with their partially consumed breakfast and coffees before them. Everyone looked as tired, and almost as grumpy, as himself.

"What the hell is going on? Who scratched up our lounge room walls? They were freshly painted now it's all got to be done again," he yelled.

Several pairs of eyes regarded him with disdain. They all turned back to their breakfast.

Elijah's temper hit boiling point. "Well? Who did it?" he shouted.

Brad sat back in his seat, took a sip of coffee and spoke up. "Mate, you should see our place. Some bastard scratched up our walls and tried to rip the handle off our bedroom door. If we hadn't locked it, they'd have got in and who knows what then," he said.

"How the hell?" Elijah said.

Chris piped up, "They got in through our lounge. The bay windows weren't locked. Damn police. They did a beaut number finishing the demo in the lounge room, but then they tore up the hallway walls and our bedroom door."

"I heard them but thought it was Chris. This place is too noisy at night," said Mischa.

"The cops were pretty pissed. Gave Doug a real reaming over it," said Chris.

Elijah slumped down in a spare seat next to Chris.

Chris smiled, slapped him on the shoulder and said, "Don't worry too much. Dougie and Ayesha have given us a few days off until this whole body thing blows over. You can bugger off home or spend some time working on your apartment. Your choice mate."

Elijah stared at him for a moment without speaking.

Chris picked up his empty cup and rose from his seat. He showed the cup to Elijah. "Coffee?"

Doug hunkered down at the entrance to where the hollow had stood. He held a metre-long piece of reinforcing steel and moved it through the piles of dirt and dust on the floor. The fine powder yielded nothing but more dust.

"It's not there is it?" asked a voice from behind.

Doug dropped the steel rod in surprise. He stood up and faced the owner of the voice.

Standing behind him, Ayesha studied Doug's search area. "I'd be shocked if whoever did this to him, left it lying around."

Doug shook his head, "Yeah. I've found nothing. If that body was him, it should be nearby." Doug stood and wiped his hands on his pants.

Ayesha indicated the broken brickwork, "I've been wondering if this was done by one of his followers. Someone who knows the legend and is after the same thing."

"Would anyone remember? It's been over a hundred years."

"There are a large group of nutters out there who still keep his legend alive. They talk about the amulet all the time. Not just because it's valuable but they say it was his power," she said.

"How do you know all this?" Doug asked.

"Internet dude, internet. How else?"

He peered across at the exit from the basement lounge room. "We'll have to get those doors secured. Can't have any bastard waltzing in here. Too much expensive equipment," he said.

"And the contestants," Ayesha suggested.

"Oh, yeah, right. The contestants. Can't forget them," he said, a wide grin on his face. He turned back to the damaged wall and sighed. "We got this place for a bargain because of the legend, but I didn't really think we'd find anything," he said.

"Is that why you put a clause in all the contracts that says anything found is the property of the producers?" Ayesha said.

"Well, yeah, on the chance that one of those idiots found the necklace and tried to keep it, we'd sue their asses off."

Ayesha stepped up to the hollow and looked all around it. "It's a shame. All we've got is a body. In a wall. With a demon binding symbol on the wall," she said as she turned back toward Doug.

He mouthed "What?"

"Yeah, I checked that too. It doesn't mean it was Walter Thurley. It doesn't mean it was the most evil man to live in nineteenth century Australia. A man suspected of the ritual deaths of over ten young women. A man whose hedonistic tastes would shock even the Marquis de Sade. No, it doesn't mean that, does it?"

Doug gave her a withering look.

Ayesha simply smiled. "The necklace is long gone. Whoever killed him and put him behind this wall has it," she said as she walked out.

Petra stared at the necklace one last time before placing it in the safe. It seemed to shine with a brilliance all its own and she felt there was a power emanating from it that vibrated down her arm.

She shut the safe door just as Elijah returned.

"What are you doing?" he asked.

She looked up at him and smiled. "Just checking our stuff is safe. Whoever did that damage outside might have come in here while we were sleeping," she said.

Elijah harrumphed. "Bastards," he said, "They wrecked everyone else's place too. It'll take us all day to fix and repaint those walls."

Petra stood. "Well we better get to it then," she said.

Elijah nodded, an angry look still on his face. He turned and walked out of the bedroom.

Petra took one last look at the safe, a feeling of despair at leaving the necklace ran through her body. She shook it off and joined Elijah outside.

Just as Brad dragged his paint roller over the last bit of wall damaged by the previous night's intruder, Chris stepped into the lounge room and admired the paint job while Brad finished.

"Good job man, wanna come and do ours when it's finished?" he asked.

"Get stuffed." Came Brad's joking reply. "You won't be ready for a week anyway. Unless you find another body then it'll be two."

Chris laughed, "Yeah, true. About that, the rest of us are gonna head down to the pub for a meal and a couple of beers. Our shout. We caused all this crap so thought it only fair."

"Dude, you found a body in a wall. Nothing you could have done about that," Brad replied.

"Yeah, but any excuse for a bit of a piss up, right?"

"We'll take a rain check. Gonna head home to see the kids. We've almost finished in here and can't do much until the furniture arrives in a couple of days. So, thanks, but no thanks," said Brad.

"Kids. Gotta be hard that. Leavin' them to be here."

But it should make it much easier for us.

Chris smiled at the thought. "You enjoy then. See ya in a few days," Chris said before leaving.

Shelley walked in from the other end of the apartment. "What was that?" she asked.

"The others are going down the pub. If you wanna push off in the morning I thought it'd be better if we didn't go."

Shelley's face changed to a lascivious grin. "Do you mean that the whole place will be empty? No people? No cameras? Nothing?"

Brad took a moment then realised what she meant. His face split into a wide grin too. "Yeah, I reckon it will."

As the competitors from *Flat Out Renos* sat back after a sumptuous meal and enjoyed their third round of drinks, their apartment block lay silent in the darkness. Only one set of lights were ablaze at the ground floor entrance, all others were dark.

Inside, only the odd ticking and creak from the building could be heard as it settled; the cold of night weaving through its old bones.

Except on the second level.

Grunts, groans and sighs of pleasure emanated from the closed bedroom. The couple inside engaged in pure release after the weeks of hard work endured to raise their apartment from derelict to a glorious standard of living.

They failed to hear the scraping as dead fingers scored deep into the freshly filled and painted plasterboard of their lounge room and hallway. Withered feet stepped and tapped across the wooden panelling of the floors and finally stopped outside of the rutting room.

An ancient hand, more bones wrapped in leather than flesh, grasped at the door handle and pushed down. The latch let go and the door swung silently inwards revealing the naked back of the man as he moved rhythmically in his wife's embrace. The woman's head was thrust back in pleasure, her eyes shut in delight.

The walking corpse stepped into the room, the carpet deadening the sound of its feet.

Its hollow eye sockets regarded the copulating pair with intense interest. Its emaciated brain drew upon decades old memories and fired with delight at the hedonistic display, but its instincts drew its focus back to the mission.

It stepped up to the bed and thrust its dagger like fingers deep into the back of the naked man. He screamed in agony and reared back. The woman's eyes snapped open. Her matching scream pierced through the silence of the apartment building.

The cadaver pulled the screaming man up towards its face. It gazed at him with a vacant expression. There was no evidence of what it sought. It brought up its free hand and plunged two skinless fingers into the man's eyes and through into his brain. The struggling man went still. He was dropped in a lifeless heap as the corpse turned its attention to the naked woman before it.

She screamed herself hoarse and her brain started to retreat into insanity. She tried to claw away from the rotting vision before her, but found the wall blocking her.

The corpse stepped around the man's body and leapt towards her, its hands thrust forward, its mouth opened wide.

The woman's last thoughts were *there are worse things than death. There are teeth.*

The light from Doug's torch cast a sickly yellow pall over the exposed stonework of the basement apartment's wall.

That damn necklace has to be here somewhere.

Doug kicked at a brick lying in the middle of the room. His steel capped boots sent it skidding across the floor with a sharp scraping sound. He stopped, dead still and listened.

Nothing.

Still at the pub. Good. Plenty of time to search.

He scanned the lounge area before moving off into the depths of the apartment. The kitchen, bedrooms and bathrooms held no interest. Ayesha and he had investigated them when they first bought the building. They had been ravaged by time and intruders, probably

Thurley's followers. There was one feature he'd always found strange but had never taken much notice of; until the discovery of the hollow.

Stepping through a doorway, into the shared corridor, he focused the torch on the grotesque fountain that sat just outside in the tiny communal courtyard on the east side of the apartment block.

The statue was a bull-headed demon entwined with a human woman. The beast's man-like physique showed it quite ready to join with the woman. Ayesha believed that Thurley had commissioned the sculpture to embrace his love for the pagan god Moloch. The model used for the woman turned up dead many years before Thurley disappeared. Suspicion was raised that she had been a ritual sacrifice. Part of a long string of unsolved murders. Accusations had flown, but there had never been enough evidence to lay charges against Thurley or his congregation.

There were rumours that the fountain sat over the original well used to water the beef cattle and drovers that frequented the pub, but it had been filled in when the towers were built.

Doug placed his torch down and focused the beam onto the fountain. He grabbed the nearby sledgehammer in both hands and swung it towards the monstrous carving.

The statue shattered with one blow. The human figurine exploding into tiny pieces, the bullhead falling to the side, to stare back at Doug with a malevolent grin on its face. The torch emphasising the wickedness of its expression.

Doug sneered and stepped forward. The head burst as the sledgehammer pulverised it into tiny pieces.

He looked back at the fountain and saw the beginning of a sizeable gap at the base. Several swings revealed the hole in its entirety. He pushed the debris away with his boots. A few pieces fell into the cavity and dropped away into the abyss, the sound of them hitting water far below echoed towards him. The chasm was deep; much deeper than made sense. He realised the old well had never been filled.

Doug picked up the torch and shone it into the hole. The beam wasn't strong enough to reach the bottom. "Jesus," Doug said. "What the hell is down there?"

A voice like the wind rustling through a cemetery replied from behind Doug. "Not hell. Heaven," it said.

Doug spun around. The torch lit up the speaker. Doug screamed.

Thurley's corpse stood before him. Fresh blood spattered the parchment skin of its face and chest. Its teeth were bared and flecked with blood and bits of flesh.

"What the fuck?" Doug cried.

Thurley stepped forward and grabbed Doug by the throat. He dragged the larger man towards him and stared deep into his soul with his hollow eye sockets. "Where is it?" he rasped.

"Where's what?" Doug said.

Thurley brought Doug closer.

The director smelt the grave and gagged on the cloying odour.

"The necklace? It is gone. Where?"

"I don't know. I was looking for it. Maybe it's down there," he said.

"Then help me find it," the corpse said. It lifted Doug up with surprising ease and shoved him headfirst into the hole. He slipped through easily and fell for an eternity. His scream echoed through the void, cut off as his neck snapped on the rocks lying beneath the shallow pool.

Noises from the front of the building grabbed Thurley's attention. Voices. Talking loudly. Singing. The others returning to the building. The corpse padded off into the uninhabited bowels of the apartment block in readiness for its next move.

"The necklace of Moloch. A thin gold chain holding a solid gold medallion with an onyx centre inlaid with the golden head of a bull. The eyes of the bull were of the purest diamond. Extremely expensive in intrinsic value, but priceless to those who believed in its power. Moloch was the Canaanite god of sacrifice and resurrection." Ayesha read out loud to herself.

She pored over the detailed content on the latest website she'd unearthed. Seated at her dining table, her computer shone a sickly hue across her face. A TV in the corner played silently, casting its glow across one side of the room.

She scrolled down the page and stopped at a paragraph detailing the powers of the necklace.

Argus of Carthage wrote that the necklace could bring the dead back to life or bring immortality to the wearer, she read. Her face was incredulous as she pushed herself back from the table.

"That's bull. These people are just superstitious idiots," she said to the computer. She crossed her arms in rejection of the article and tried to look away. Her eyes were immediately drawn back to the article. She bent forward and began to read again.

The last known location of the necklace was Australia. It had been stolen from a crypt beneath the Palais des Papes in Avignon France in 1845 but had shown up around the neck of Walter Thurley in 1879.

The Catholic Church denied all knowledge of its existence, but it was recorded that numerous attempts to regain the necklace were carried out and Thurley avoided assassination on at least five occasions.

The location of the necklace was lost upon Thurley's disappearance in 1915. It is believed that the necklace was lost with Thurley.

"Damn," she said out loud and slumped forward to read more.

Walter Thurley migrated to Australia in 1820 and purchased the Bull's Head public house in 1840, and all its surrounding lands. The pub had existed on the site for over thirty years, servicing the drovers who brought their beef herds into Sydney for sale at the market. Thurley built a large Georgian building that was first christened Moloch Towers, but was changed to Thurley Towers soon after.

A footnote at the bottom provided an explanation.

In 1841, the local Catholic Church applied to the local magistrate to have the name of Moloch towers changed. They cited the fact that Moloch was the name of a pagan god. The magistrate agreed and the building was renamed in 1842.

Ayesha stopped reading.

Hang on, she thought, *he migrated to Australia in 1820? Even if he was twenty years old then, he would have been over a hundred years old when he disappeared. This is ridiculous.*

It was then Ayesha saw the final line. She sat bolt upright. It was Thurley's registered date of birth, 6th of June 1766.

"He was one hundred and forty-nine when he disappeared. That's ridiculous. There's no way he could be that old," she said.

Unless . . . She left the thought hanging as she scrolled down to the bottom of the page, but only found banner ads for useless ephemera.

She slumped back in her chair and stared at the screen.

None of this makes sense. No one knows where he went. The necklace must be there. If not? Why would his followers break in and try to find it?

She turned and saw a newsflash on the TV. The headline said, "Renovation show corpse stolen."

She grabbed the remote and turned up the volume. A video of a local police station was playing as the newsreader talked over it.

"The body, found on the set of reality show *Flat out Renos*, has been stolen from the city morgue. The security guards at the building are perplexed as there was no sign of a break-in. Police are investigating the security footage and have suggested it was an inside job linked to an incident on the reality TV show site yesterday."

Ayesha stared for a moment and grabbed her phone. She punched in Doug's number. The phone rang four times then went through to voicemail.

"Doug, it's Ayesha. Thurley's body has been stolen. I reckon it's his followers. They'll probably try to break into the building again. You've got to warn the competitors. We should get them out of there until this all blows over."

She started another sentence, but the voicemail beep signalled, and the phone cut off.

She put the mobile down and bumped her wireless mouse. The pointer flew across and rested on a small hyperlink on the screen. A popup appeared with the demon binding symbol she'd seen carved into the wall of Thurley's burial chamber.

Intrigued she clicked on the link and a page detailing the symbol appeared.

Beneath a drawing of the symbol it said.

Asmodeus binding Sigel. A powerful symbolic mark purportedly used by the arch-demon Asmodeus to bind the god Moloch to Earth until the time of judgement.

Ayesha stared at the screen and quickly read the rest of the blurb. When she finished a light sheen of perspiration had appeared on her forehead. She stood up.

If these idiots believe this crap, they'll do anything to get him back.

"Shit—the competitors!" she shouted.

A black and white blur flew from the couch, stopping a couple of metres away and looking back with confused eyes.

Ayesha realised she'd frightened her cat with her outburst. She changed tone and held a hand towards to the animal, "I'm sorry puss, did I do it again? Mommy was worried about some people."

The cat padded closer and lifted her head up for a pat.

"Now, I've got to go. You be good and no surfing cat porn, okay?"

In the ground floor bedroom, Ivan laid on his back and snored away obliviously. Mischa had become used to her well-built husband's sleeping patterns, she normally beat him into dreamland and escaped the tortuous buzz saw howl, but tonight's drinking session had curtailed her escape. She rolled over and away from his snores and clamped her eyes shut. The first vestiges of her inevitable hangover had already surfaced, and sleep was going to be a long shot.

A drop of liquid smacked onto her cheek. Her eyes flashed open and looked around in the dark. She brought her hand to her cheek. The sticky liquid smeared across her face.

That's not water.

Another drop. Her hand shot out and grabbed for her phone. She switched on the torch and looked at her hand. The liquid left a red stain on her fingers. She turned on the camera and looked at her reflection. Her face was smeared in red.

What the?

She shone the torch onto the ceiling to look for the source. A large red stain had spread across it.

Paint? Goddamn it. Those idiots upstairs have knocked over a tin of paint. They were probably screwing while the rest of us were at the pub.

She elbowed Ivan. "Wake up you big buffoon."

Ivan snorted, rolled over and continued to chainsaw his way through another dream.

"Fine." Mischa quickly dressed and made her way to the upstairs apartment. She used her phone to light the way and stopped outside of Brad and Shelley's bedroom to raise enough anger in herself.

She grabbed the door handle, thrust open the door and switched on the light.

The sight shocked her to her soul. Her phone dropped to the carpet and bounced away. Her hands went to her face in disbelief. Her mouth opened ready to scream but nothing would come out but a silent croak.

A noise made her spin around and away from the blood-soaked carnage on the bedroom floor.

The sight before her was no better. She finally screamed as she saw the animated corpse of Walter Thurley.

Thurley thrust a hand out and caught Mischa by the throat. He pushed her up against the nearest wall and lifted her upwards until her feet kicked out at thin air. "Where is it?" Thurley gasped.

"Where is what?" Mischa managed to croak out through her crushed windpipe.

Thurley moved closer. Mischa stared into the deep, rotted holes of the corpse's eyes. "Where is the necklace?"

Mischa's eyes opened impossibly wide in confusion. "What necklace?"

Thurley stood perfectly still. His vacant expression fixed on Mischa's gaping eyes, peering deep into her soul for the answers he sought.

Finally, he spoke. "You know nothing," he whispered. He twisted his hand. A dry, brittle crack snapped out across the apartment.

Mischa's eyes rolled back. Her head hung to the side at a terrible angle.

Thurley dropped her body in a heap and moved towards the stairway.

Petra stood near the towering glass windows of the penthouse's master bedroom and stared out over the city lights twinkling in the clear night. She peeled off her clothes and let them fall in a heap near her feet. Several glasses of wine had left her with a happy internal glow. She stood and bathed in the cool breeze floating in through the open doorway that lead out onto the penthouse's balcony.

She went to the safe and extracted the bull's head necklace. It was heavy around her neck, but the coolness of the metal against her skin felt wonderful.

Removing the last vestiges of clothing, Petra stared naked at the world beyond, waiting for Elijah to return. She wanted to cap the night off in the best of ways.

A noise at the doorway made her turn.

"Hello lover," Petra said to the silhouette that filled the entrance.

The figure stood stock still and regarded her.

"Elijah?" Petra peered closer and realised the shape was slimmer and shorter than Elijah.

It stepped forward.

She saw it definitely wasn't Elijah.

"Who are you?" She tried to cover herself with her hands.

The figure stepped further into the room. A shaft of reflected moonlight fell across its face and exposed her mistake.

Petra screamed as the corpse's details were revealed.

It regarded her with its hollow eye sockets and spied the necklace. It raised a withered hand towards her.

"Mine," it hissed and took two steps towards her.

"Hey," Elijah shouted and stepped into the room. The corpse turned at the sound. Elijah walked up to the dead man and raised a fist to pummel it.

"What the hell are you doing here?"

The corpse was faster and ducked the blow, bringing its clawed hand up into the man's stomach. The bony fingers pierced the flesh and the hand buried itself deep in Elijah's insides. Thurley dragged a fistful of intestines back out and let them flop to the carpeted floor.

Petra screamed.

Elijah's hands went to the hole in his abdomen in a vain attempt to hold his organs in place as they spilled to the floor. His head dropped to stare at the pile at his feet and he fell to his knees amongst them. His last act was to stare up at his attacker.

The corpse thrust its outstretched fingers deep into the man's eyes. Thurley pulled his hand back and flicked an eyeball to the floor as Elijah fell forwards into the steaming pile of guts and lay still.

Petra stopped screaming long enough to take in what had just happened. She looked at the corpse as it turned towards her. She wanted to scream some more but nothing would come out.

Thurley held up a blood-soaked hand and pointed at the necklace. "Give to me."

Petra looked down at the necklace and back at the body of her dead husband. She felt the cool breeze on her back and stepped out through the open doorway and onto the balcony. She looked around and spied the doorway into the living room. She quickly padded across the cold concrete on bare feet and grabbed the handle.

Locked.

"Why the hell is this locked?" she shouted.

A clicking noise came from behind her.

She spun.

The corpse had stepped onto the balcony through the only other exit.

Petra had one chance, she grabbed at the necklace, tore it off, held it out in front of her and shouted, "Is this what you want?"

Petra moved to the edge of the balcony.

The skeletal feet scraped across the concrete, as the corpse closed in on her.

"Come on," she said. Holding the necklace at arms-length, she stepped closer to the edge, keeping her eyes on the corpse.

As she took another step, she screamed as her foot exploded in blinding pain. She looked down and saw several nails poking up through her foot. Blood poured out through the wounds.

Petra's memory blazed with the image of the old paling from the external wall tossed carelessly aside. Pain clouded her mind as she denigrated herself for her stupidity.

All was forgotten as a clawed hand grabbed her throat.

The necklace came free and dropped from her hand towards the courtyard below.

Thurley's corpse let out an exasperated gasp of fetid breath as it watched the golden medallion disappear below. It turned its rotted head towards Petra. "You follow," it gasped.

Petra's eyes widened.

Thurley grabbed her between the legs and hoisted her into the air.

She screamed as she was launched over the balcony's edge and fell towards the ground. Her last vision was of the spiked finials of the wrought iron fence rushing to greet her.

Ayesha parked in the side road next to the apartment block. She stepped out of the car and looked around. Only a couple of lights burned in the building. Peering through the wrought iron fence she tried to discern any movement in the darkened basement apartment.

She pulled out her phone and rang Doug's number. A familiar tune rang out into the night. She stared into the communal courtyard and saw a small flashing light next to the demolished fountain. The intermittent flashing barely illuminated the site of Doug's renovation.

"Doug what have you done?" She tapped on the phone's torch function and shone it across the area.

Doug's sledgehammer lay near the open hole beneath the fountain. Broken masonry and brick was strewn around it.

"Doug? Where are you?"

A glint of gold flashed in the beam and disappeared.

Ayesha shone the torch on the ground and saw a gold necklace lying in the rubble. "That's it!"

A scream pierced the night. She looked up and saw a figure falling towards her.

Ayesha jumped back as Petra fell onto the wrought iron fence.

The finials slammed through her torso and burst out of her chest. Her head hung back and her dying eyes stared at Ayesha in disbelief. Petra's last act was to point upwards.

Ayesha looked in the same direction and saw a dark, indistinct figure peering over the balcony of the penthouse. Her first thoughts were of Petra's husband. "Elijah?" she shouted.

When the figure ducked back without answering, Ayesha realised the worst. "They're here!" She shone the torch back towards the necklace.

She rushed down the stairs into the basement courtyard. The only access to the communal courtyard was through the shared corridor inside. The basement apartment's courtyard doors were locked.

Ayesha stepped back and kicked with her heavy work boots. Chris and Jenna had been stingy, the door burst open on the third try.

Ayesha made her way through the lounge room, peering at the remains of Thurley's crypt before moving into the main part of the apartment.

As she ducked down the hallway towards the side entrance, Jenna appeared in the bedroom doorway. "Ayesha?" she said.

Ayesha turned. "We need to get out of here now. There are people here. Petra's dead," she mumbled.

Jenna stepped out towards her. "What? Petra's dead? What are you talking about?" she said.

Chris followed her out. His mind still deep in sleep despite being awake and standing. "Was goin' on?" he said.

"No time to explain. Come with me now. We need to get out of here," Ayesha said urging them on.

Chris replied, "Bugger that 'm goin' back to bed."

Jenna nodded in agreement and started to turn. She stopped short as a piece of reinforcing steel burst through Chris' chest showering her in blood.

Chris looked down at the rod, mouthed a couple of words then collapsed to his knees revealing Thurley's corpse standing behind him.

Jenna screamed.

Ayesha grabbed her by the shoulders and dragged her away. They ran down the hallway and out through the side entrance.

Jenna stumbled into the courtyard. Her wide-eyed expression peered out of her blood-spattered face.

Ayesha jammed a piece of wood across the glass doors to hold them shut but was unconvinced they would stop anything. She stepped over and grabbed the necklace out of the dirt. It glinted in the limited light with its own inner radiance.

Jenna's shattered mind managed to string words together and said, "Chris is dead. That. That thing killed him. What is it?"

Ayesha turned towards her. Confusion and fear playing across her own face. "I thought it was just some guy after this." She held up the necklace. "But I think it's the corpse you guys found."

"The what?"

"The dead body. From the wall. The one you found."

"No. No. No. That's impossible," she said, shaking her head and hugging herself for comfort.

"You'd think but . . ."

The sound of smashing glass broke Ayesha's comeback. Thurley broke through the window with the steel rod still soaked in Chris' blood and reached through to remove the wooden beam.

Ayesha ran over and grabbed the sledgehammer. She picked it up and hefted its weight onto her shoulder. "Come and get some," she hollered in an act of defiance rather than bravery.

Thurley threw the wood aside and burst out into the courtyard. He turned towards Ayesha and held out his hand. "Give to me. I will grant you everlasting life or else I will give you a quick death."

Ayesha stepped back towards the fountain and looked into the hole below. It seemed to go on forever. She held her hand out and hung the necklace over the hole. "Come and get it," she said, taunted the corpse.

Thurley stepped forward, raising the steel rod as he approached.

Jenna stood nearby, shaking in abject fear. She looked from the corpse to Ayesha, trying to digest what was happening. She stared at the broken fountain, then looked away and saw a long pry bar leaning against a wall. She quickly stepped over, picked it up and felt the weight. Her confusion evaporated in her mind. A small grin came to her lips.

As Thurley closed in on Ayesha he swung the rod in a wide arc, taking Ayesha by surprise.

The necklace was knocked from her grasp and dropped to the ground next to the hole.

In his hurry to regain his prize, Thurley dropped the steel pole and went to his knees.

Jenna ran from behind him and slammed the pry bar into his bony back. Thurley fell forward and slid headfirst into the hole. Ayesha brought the sledgehammer down and sent him plummeting into the depths below. A rage filled scream filled with obscenities coursed up from the pit.

Ayesha looked around for something to cover the hole. A large flat block of concrete lay nearby. She motioned for Jenna to help her and both managed to drag the slab over and cover the hole. She pulled out her phone and scrolled through the photos. A discarded screwdriver became her scribe and she quickly scored the surface with the demon binding seal. As soon as she completed the design the screams from below stopped.

Ayesha sat down on a small pile of bricks and wiped the sweat from her forehead. "Fuck," she said.

Jenna stood staring at the seal for a moment then tears sprung from her eyes and coursed down her cheeks.

Ayesha moved closer and took the girl in her arms.

Jenna's sobs petered out after a few moments and she blinked the tears away. She saw the necklace sitting in the dirt near the concrete slab and turned to Ayesha. "What are you gonna do with that?"

Ayesha turned and noticed the golden glint. She stepped over to it and looked down. "I could still sell it, like Doug and I planned."

"Or not," said Jenna.

Ayesha looked at her and nodded. "Yeah. I think you're right. Give me a hand."

Jenna stepped over to the slab and helped her lift it.

Ayesha slid the necklace towards the hole and pushed it over the edge. It slid out of sight and made a small plopping sound as it hit the water below. No other sound greeted them as they dropped the slab back into place.

Ayesha stepped back and turned to view the apartment block.

"What do we do now?" asked Jenna.

A look of regret swept over Ayesha's face. "I'm thinking a bulldozer and a lot of concrete. Nobody's been interested in this place for over a hundred years, hopefully no one will ever be again," she said.

STEPHEN HERCZEG

About the Author:

Stephen is an IT Geek, writer, actor, film maker and Taekwondo Black Belt based in Canberra Australia. He has been writing for over twenty years and has completed a couple of dodgy novels, sixteen feature length screenplays and dozens of short stories and scripts.

Stephen's scripts TITAN, Dark are the Woods, Control *and* Death Spores *have found success in international screenwriting competitions with a win, two runner-up and two top ten finishes.*
His horror stories have featured in various anthologies including: Sproutlings; Hells Bells; Trickster's Treats #1, #2 and #3; Shades of Santa; Below the Stairs; Behind the Mask; Beyond the Infinite; Beside the Seaside; The Body Horror Book; Anemone Enemy; Petrified Punks; Beginnings; Sea of Secrets, Demonic Carnival; Deep Space; A Tribute to H.G. Wells; What If?; Through Death's Door *and* Coffins and Dragons.

Over forty of his drabbles have been accepted by Blood Song Books; Black Hare Press; Fantasia Divinity and ThingsInTheWell.

Several of his Sherlock Holmes pastiches have been accepted for inclusion in anthologies published by Belanger Books and MX Publishing.

You can catch Stephen at his Facebook page:
https://www.facebook.com/stephenherczegauthor

Meet Me By The Moon When I'm Flicking Through A Cheap Magazine Talking About Astrology

Brianna Bullen

There is nothing more inconvenient than to love when one is fated to die. We attach ourselves to others at the worst of times, making kinships out of borrowed time and late-night whispered dirges, barely audible over the vacant hum of the ship and our laboured breathing. The air down here feels toxic through the nose. There is little oxygen here. Pressed up against each other, shoulder to shoulder, we consume each other's carbon dioxide as if it were food. In the lower rungs of the ship, we are allocated little in the way of air supply or comfort.

What we are given is hay. Hay, cruelty and—strangely—books. Little paperbacks to give us a 'moral education' and to mock us. Asterion, Asterion, Asterion. Borges' story repeated as mocking litany, again and again, pacing inside our heads. None of us are mindless monsters. With clipboards and a checklist, they monitor our progress and neural waves—are these creatures registering our words? How complex can we go? Dr Seuss or Tolstoy? Realism or the existential fantastic? Orwellian dystopic lives. How to measure them using theories of development if they cannot speak? A biped with the title scientist visits us every few rotations. I have given up measuring it through the release of food through the chutes above. The scientist comes at irregular intervals. It makes it harder to breathe, all of us tense, large lungs afraid to heave for fear of drawing attention at the wrong moment.

A new calf has been born. The biped has been down more regularly as of late to check on its progress. The creature is a runt; a mewling, baying thing with terrified eyes and flared nostrils. It stomps at the ground with the self-righteous audacity of a child, looking for an exit with nowhere to run. We were all born this way. The child will soon know it is not special, will be as still and silent as the rest of us.

His mother is an older cow with sad grey eyes, hunched over shoulders and a weak back. Her ear tag has a list of numbers that those with cerebral enhancements can read but do not tell her what they mean. If numbers are designations for humans, I refuse them. We refer to her as Mother, and before that, Key, as the pattern on her rump matches the adornments of our captors. There are many in our sad herd, but she is the cellmate placed by my side, and the one I am fondest of. The calf could be mine, or it could be one of any of the bulls. Extraction and insemination is entirely artificial. The touch we get is only from metal and the bruising rub of shoulders shoved too close together in not enough space.

I have a tag pierced through my own ear, a dandelion yellow. I only know of dandelions from a freak mix-up in the seeds meant for our food. I have not seen anything so beautiful nor delicate since they removed the few stowaway flowers. The number is not important, but the tag claps against my ear, I can feel its touch on my neck like a fly with every step I am privileged to make or every shake of the head. It is another sound effect I use to distract myself whenever the tension is too much. The other bovines call me "Lucky" in both their rudimentary human words and in their eyes. I was one of the few the neural operations worked well on. "Predisposition from the genetic modification of the parents," the scientist and his own flock once muttered, and it stuck with me. Stuck like the scars sealing over my head where they cut open my skull to prod needles, scalpels and tubes in my brain, hoping to "enhance and unlock potential" with brutality and quackery. Hacksaw through horn and bone.

Cud crawls up from stomach through throat and back into my mouth. I ruminate on it, chewing every now and again. My ears are pricked, anticipating the door to open at any moment. There's a drop of sweat running down my shoulder, stinging hot skin with chill. My hooves are pace-begging, but there is no room. Every nerve cell and hair on my body seems to be pulsing on end. My heartbeat barrels through its heavy-set chest—or am I hearing the anxiety of any number of my herd? Moments of terror mobilise empathy. A network connection, everyone attuned to the same frequency.

It is hard to measure days in a windowless room, no less a windowless room in the depths of space. Light is a luxury, even when it is dim and artificial. But I think it's a harvest day, one where the biped crew in the surrounding rooms feast on the flesh of one of our own. We are a resource kept not just for the idle fancy and experiments of bored scientists, but for the meals of the wealthiest crewmembers every few months. They needed to ensure we were living in "sustainable" amounts, rather than taking up too many resources, "human intelligence" or no.

I'd fear for my kin if I wasn't also relieved for whoever was chosen. The cud goes back down my throat as I swallow. Someone moos behind me, a forlorn sound. It is impossible to tell who began the cry as the dirge is soon added to from every angle. It bounces off the metal walls. At least twenty voices are calling out—loudly, screaming, crying and wanting to be recognised as suffering. I feel each soul through the ground, through my hooves. Even the calf stops its incessant suckling and halts all movement, as if caught in a tractor beam. Its innocence will end as soon as one of its companions is bolted through the head. I keep my eyes on its cheerful pair. It will know no better than these first few months.

I do not join the song of my peers; no sound can pass on what I fear.

We hear the scientist before we see them today. A cooing sound we now know is condescending but would previously have been soothed by. "Hello, my lovelies." They start humming a song which creeps beneath the door and into our bones. The door takes a while to unlock, but we can hear each bolt being moved with finality before the handle is turned with a dropping whine. Metal screams with regularity. The scientist pokes their head through, glasses fogged up by coffee steam, but I can still see the laughter in their steel eyes. It's the one with the matted hair today. They've taken one step into the room and already they're tugging through dark hair, scratching at their scalp. Even cruel people seem to have habits they want to break.

Today, the scientist has several glasses and a torch balanced on their book. It's a thick textbook today, even though I can't make out the title. It's all in the shape, overstuffed with facts and definitions, with some glossy photos which make little darker lines in the pages' sides.

"Alright my bovine beauties, today we are going to be taking a page out of Piaget." They put down the book and holds the glasses behind their back. "Stomp your feet if the glass is still present."

There's a frenzied stamping from the herd. Many understand his words; the others know to follow the actions of those that react. The calf bleats in alarm as his mother stomps, eyes white. Following too slowly or not at all increases the risk of being on the chopping block. Our regular handler has also slipped through the door. From the bolt-gun at his side, we know he is bringing neither food or care. Luckily for the calf, no others bleed into the room from the gap in the door. It is strange, but it sometimes happens that they lead one of our number out into the foyer outside where a team is waiting to kill it and disassemble the body. Less stench and panic and bodies to manoeuvre through. Greater efficiency, minimal panic, less chance that the cow will escape than if they led it into wherever it is that they prepare food.

The scientist sometimes mocks us with our history, speaks of ramps and houses made for our slaughter, says that we're "a lucky bunch of fat cows" as if they've forgotten they've taught us how to listen to their words.

"So that's a resounding understanding of object permanence," the handler mutters as they check our water levels, drawing more for us with the switch of a high-up button. Had it been any lower, I know I would have been tempted to press against it. Waste more of their water from our allotment. But it would only have punished us.

"Hm, maybe Jo." the scientist slaps an older heifer on the shoulder, feels down its leg and manoeuvres it in a circle to check for movement. "Or herd mentality. One knows, the rest follow."

The handler scoffs. Pulls a face after the first sentence. I don't know why they do this.

The heifer gets praised by the scientist who then moves onto the next. "Do you mind filling that tall slim glass for me? Got to make sure they still understand conservation principles."

The handler grumbles but complies. "Don't know why you have to do this so much. They know. That's not going to change."

"Oh no, regression is entirely possible. Would be annoying after all this time—interesting and a new direction for study, but annoying."

"You ever going to get them to speak?" The handler scratches their neck. There are no flies in the ship, but the sweat-damp air creeps across the skin, stings the senses. Flies remain a story, told across generations. At least there aren't any flies, the old Earth-born cows had said. Annoying miniscule creatures that latched onto the side and stung.

The scientist titters.

The handler laughs. The sound is a cruel growl, loud and slightly awkward as if expecting discipline from the noise. "Stupid of me, I know. What would a cow even have to say? Nothing of any value, surely."

The scientist turns to them. I can't see their gaze or expression, but it causes the handlers to freeze and then drop.

"It'd be my dream to hear if they have anything to say. I only laugh in the face of the task as it seems momentous, too large for someone so simple. I'm just imagining the operations I'd need to do to get their larynxes and brain capable of the task—too traumatic. They would not want to speak to us after that kind of torture. No, it'd be enough if we could get them to understand us. To understand themselves."

The handler shakes their head. "Don't think there's much to understand there. Maybe just moo, shit, smelly, food, yum, water, drink, walk, danger. Might not even be able to understand danger if I'm honest."

The scientist pushes up their glasses. "Honest for what you know, not honest of the actual truth. Can't you see their nerves? Feel it in their sides, the tension in their backs, the snorting of their nostrils? They understand fear."

"Upper management know that?"

"Wouldn't let me keep a herd with our limited resources if they didn't."

It's strange. I hear these words. I know these words as individual units from the stories this person tells us. Can stitch them together to try and comprehend what they mean in the sequence spoken. But often I do not understand. I do not understand, because I do not understand these creatures, or this strange land of humming air and engines that we find ourselves in.

"Do you think any of this lot will ever touch down on Kep?"

"This lot? They'd be pushing it." The scientist walks over to the calf beside me. It shivers, buries itself beneath its mother as much as it can. Smart child. The scientist coos and rubs its mother's shivering side, trying to coax movement. "Next generation should, though. Just got to check your baby, sweetheart. Thatta girl."

Their words of comfort trickle as poison, some chloroform or relaxant that forces your guard down however much you struggle against it. The shuddering calf peeks out, face still half-tucked away. It's reached for, and it flinches back.

"Relax little buddy," the handler came over to assist, coaxing the baby out. "The captain doesn't want veal tonight, you're safe."

I feel my hair stand on end. How dare they threaten a child who doesn't understand. The calf squeals and hides deeper underneath its mother. Smart kid. They laugh. Why are they laughing?

The lesson today is truncated. The humans clearly hunger. The calf's mother is sleepy-eyed, more milky than present. She falters on the mathematics tasks, reaction time slower and the amount of hoof beats off by one, which she slowly corrects after a deathly pause.

My own task when they get to me is literary. They hook me up to a machine, putting a cap with little spore-like buds against my scalp. They read to me. Measure my emotional responses on a handheld screen in the areas activated in my brain. It's a simpler story today, one of ill-fated friends on opposing sides in a war who meet under the cover of darkness. They play naughts and crosses in the dirt on the ground. Talk about what they'll do when the battle is over. Then one dies on the field, and the other returns to their hidden enclave and waits until morning with no response. Their marks on the ground have been dusted over in the wind. I don't understand any of it. Why bother befriending an enemy? Why risk being caught and shot? Why the mundane tasks? It's confusing, but they seem to like my responses.

Apparently confusion is a sufficient emotional response when it comes to pondering humanity to allow me to live another few months.

It was the bull in the corner, the one who often shivered and snorted with barely concealed hate, that set himself up to die. Stubborn bastard refused to so much as face the scientist, turning his head to the corner of the room and presenting his backside with a kick of the hay beneath him. His tail flicks up as he shits on the ground. The scientist laughs nervously and looks at the handler who shrugs.

"Kinda like this one's personality. He's an utter dick."

The scientist chuckles harder at the comment, mutters in low tones, "so maybe veal tonight after all?"

The words rock through me, freeze me in place. My heart thunders regardless of my body's stillness, jackhammer in a rock. How dare they. How dare they.

I wasn't aware I had moved. Wasn't aware I had gored the handler. All I was aware of was my own mind and heart, clinging to the word "unfair, unfair, unfair.'

My body barrels as a bullet to the door, knocking down and trampling the scientist who had scrambled in fear to open it. The opening is there. I part it further as I birth myself into my new life as a bull on the run. I run, and run.

I leave my family by fate behind me. I can not look back. Do not look back. I do not hear them gain the courage to follow.

Panic. Sheer panic. My soul seems to run before me, carrying my breath, and my body lumbers after it. No door can stop me, and for the first few rooms, no door does. The human pair had left the latches unlocked, to save them the minimal effort on the way out of our first heavily locked room. The doors part under my weight, before I even have time to register them; I hear only the ghost of my impact in the echoing shudder of the doors. Before I know it, I am running down a vacant corridor. Steam hisses off the side, the walls seeming to sweat as I pass a generator. Only something integral to the ship could be so loud; I avoid hitting the walls or its protrusion at all costs, slowing my pace. Temperature gauges tremor on their side, maintaining a safe range of movement. Just a flicker, then back, not a huge swing. It is damp, dark. A room barely ventured to. Lit by manual lights.

There are flickers of sound—operational buzzes, engine whines— the barest hint of movement from some stowaway pest, but otherwise it is silent. All I can hear is the heaving gasps from my barrelling chest, and the occasional howling moo of my rage. I hit an end to one corridor, I turn into the next, then the next. I am running through the labyrinth, my echoing steps my only company. If I close my eyes, I can pretend I have a herd with me. I am running for a while before my first contact with the opulence of the human beings. The corridor lights up with me, as if anticipating my movement. A reverse shadow, light protruding out before me in incremental shifts. What creatures could summon light with their own steps, demand it light their way?

There is a pair of doors before me, so different to the metal that has surrounded me all of my life. It is carved, the handles glinting. But the material—it is wood, polished and deep as the brown of my own hide. The handles curl down, long and thick as human arms, until they meet at the centre of the door's opening, like two fists side-by-side. I do not stop. The door splinters open, but I meet heavy resistance, jagged pieces embedding in my face and sides.

There are sounds of beauty I have never heard before, which seem to screech to a stop as soon as they touch my ears. On the podium, humans sat and stood holding various tools and instruments—was this an operation? What were they operating on? Each other? The air? The silence? I connect the beautiful noise with their tools as one continues beyond the rest and only jerks to a stop when their elbow is touched by a member above.

I spin around, delirious from pain and exhaustion. The adrenaline is still pumping, but the lights and the noise and the people and the smells make everything spin, triggering senses and synapse from seemingly every angle. People, even those standing still, pass in a blur. Black and white static from all the tuxedos, interrupting the usual shades of grey and muted browns. Above my head there is an upside-down tree of glittering glass. Not only does each lens catch the light, but it seems to create it. Pulse with it. Little crystal hearts. It makes me dizzier; vision flashing, melding shadow and light. The humans are eating from a trough, only it seems to be upside down with the food on top. A table? It matches the books' descriptions. Mushy peas. Carrots. Jellied cubes of protein. A banquet for those living off the essentials, with a ludicrous fountain of liquid in the centre to keep morale up. A hairless man is ladling it into his glass, but it spills over as we make eye contact. Laughter bleeds into confused whispers, morphs into delighted squeals.

A real-life animal from the decks below! What luxury was this?

I bolt through the gathering circle, splitting the shape through the centre. People leap to the ground to avoid me, while others merely side-step. My hooves click on a lacquered floor, flat feet nearly slip on the smooth stickiness as I search for a door to another room.

There is no exit.

But I am not met with a wall.

Outside is a sea of stars. Little flashing pixels. Light trying to be seen, from thousands of years away. Already dead ghosts, most of them. No less pretty. I do nothing but stare. I have never seen the sky before, but my soul and the sublime awe of stories tell me that this is such. A deeper sky, dark as oil, thick as blood. I let myself still, knowing my journey is over.

Nowhere to hide in a spaceship. My breath fogs up the window's glass and spreads its own stars from the ghost of my lungs.

About the Author:

Brianna Bullen is a Deakin University PhD creative writing candidate writing about memory in science fiction. She has had work published in journals including LiNQ, Aurealis, Voiceworks, Rabbit, Multiverse: An International Anthology of Science Fiction Poetry, *and* Woolf Pack Zine.

She won the 2017 Apollo Bay short story competition and placed second in the 2017 Newcastle Short story competition. Her manuscript was previously a finalist in the 2018 Subbed In Poetry Chapbook competition. In 2018, she was part of Nexus, an Arts Access Victoria collective for artists with mental health recovery lived experience.

THE TAUREAN

Austin P. Sheehan

In the break between school, Sophie and her parents had left their home in busy Ganima City and were spending a couple of weeks with her Uncle at his farm on the edge of the colony. Only yesterday she had watched through the viewscreens of their family's shuttle as the colony had whisked by far below, a blur of silver and grey against the pale yellow snow that covered the Ganiman surface. Her excitement about exploring the wilds beyond the farm had kept her mind racing all night, full of excitement about what she might discover.

As soon as the sun rose over the horizon, Sophie was out of bed, ready to start exploring. Dressed in her warmest clothes, she crept down the stairs, then stopped, halfway to the door. She couldn't go outside, not without her parents. Remembering the view of the mountains from last night, she went to the dining room and peered through the plascreen window. The sky was light purple, the sun would rise any minute, and the farm and the mountains beyond called to her.

With a creak, a door opened behind her.

She turned, startled, as Uncle Robb entered the house, his grey hair and broad shoulders spotted with snowflakes.

"You're up early." The warmth of his smile removed any niggling concern that she'd be in trouble for sneaking around so early.

"I couldn't sleep, I was so excited to get out and explore!"

"Well how about I give you a quick tour?"

Sophie glanced towards the stairs. "But mum and dad are still sleeping."

"Then they'll just miss out, won't they? Don't worry, it won't take long."

"Okay!" Overflowing with happiness, Sophie gave her uncle a quick hug. Robb had always been Sophie's favourite uncle, full of jokes and stories of adventure, so she was eager to go. *Maybe I'll have my own exciting story to tell when I get back to school,* she thought as her uncle's strong arms wrapped around her.

Within minutes they had sped away from the farmhouse on an e-cyce, Sophie's arms wrapping tight around her uncle. As fences, shrubs and snow-covered fields passed by in a blur, her initial twinge of fear at the thought of getting on the e-cyce disappeared. *I was silly to be scared, Uncle Robb would never let anything happen to me.*

Robb brought the e-cyce to a stop at the edge of a clearing and pointed up into the pale morning sky. A distant ship extended its landing gear, thrusters firing, and began its descent.

"Have you heard the story of the *Taurean?*" Robb asked as he stepped onto the fresh snow, then helped her off the back of the e-cyce.

Sophie smiled. *This must be one of his crazy stories.* He had been quieter than usual over dinner last night, as if he'd had something on his mind. Even when he was getting the e-cyce ready this morning she had caught her glancing at her over the handlebars with a smile, but not his usual warm smile, so her spirits lifted as he began the story. This was the Uncle Robb she remembered.

"Now this ship—designated *Taurean V*—was a transport made by Europa Prime, painted a beautiful porcelain white, and the most advanced ship of its time."

"What was so advanced about her?"

"Believe it or not, she was alive—controlled by the best Jovian AI system money could buy."

A chill ran up Sophie's spine. Everyone knew artificial intelligence couldn't be trusted. "But they can't—"

"This was a long time ago, Soph." Uncle Robb looked down at her with a comforting smile. "It was only after the rebellion of thirty-two that they outlawed AI rigs and robot crew. The stories say the *Taurean* was made in the late twenties."

Sophie smiled. The ship would have to be almost a hundred years old by now. "So what happened?"

"Well, the darndest thing. They gave her a destination and off she went."

Sophie stood still, waiting for Robb to continue as the cold creeped through her boots, through her gloves.

"Come on, this way," Robb said. "Let's keep moving so we don't freeze."

Sophie followed, trying to step into the large footprints in the snow her uncle's big boots had left behind. "But that's not so surprising," she called out after him. "About the ship taking off, I mean."

Robb turned back and nodded, slowing his pace. "True, that's what she was supposed to do. But a crew was meant to go with her, just in case anything went wrong. She was given her course remotely while they were doing the final checks, while the crew were still suiting up."

"And then?"

Robb let the question hang in the air as he reached for Sophie's hand and led her carefully across a stream and into a low valley, snow covered hills on either side. He scanned the hills as he continued the tale. "Without warning, the *Taurean* roared to life, bucking and shaking as her engines fired. People were still on the launchpad—they tried to shut her down, but it was too late. Her primary thrusters kicked in and she blasted off, incinerating the ground team."

Sophie swallowed, thinking of the horror; the agony of being burned alive. "What happened next?"

Robb shrugged. "She disappeared."

Sophie looked up at her uncle, then around at the valley. It was perfectly still, the only sounds were Robb's footsteps as he awkwardly shifted his feet, and her own breathing. Something wasn't right. She story couldn't just have ended like that.

"Is that it, Uncle? The ship was never seen again?"

"Well, not quite . . ." Robb's voice dropped as he turned to her. "The *Taurean* never landed at her programmed destination, never responded to the transmissions sent out to her. Europa Prime almost went bankrupt sending out search parties, and they never found a thing. Eventually, they guessed she'd either suffered catastrophic engine failure, tearing her apart, or her nav system malfunctioned and she went so far off-course she'll never be found."

"So she might still be lost up there, somewhere?" Sophie looked up at the faint stars visible through the thin purple atmosphere, her heart attempting to cross the unknowable divide between her and the lost ship. *Even AI systems must get lonely.*

Robb turned back to where the distant ship had landed. "No one knows for sure. But over the last few decades, reports have appeared of a mysterious white transport taking off from fields and thickets all over the galaxy." He paused, then looked at her. "And the very next day, a child is reported missing from the colony."

A chill rose through Sophie's body. Uncle Robb sounded different, cold. There was something definitely odd about him today, something *wrong.* She shivered under his gaze, searching for a way to bring back the warm, funny Robb. "But Uncle," Sophie said, forcing a smile, "she must have run out of fuel cells *ages* ago."

"You're right. But still, some folk say this mysterious ship has to be the *Taurean.* They say she goes from planet to planet and lands in empty fields, leaves her doors open, and sits in wait . . ."

Sophie imagined a ship; its small, white and round hull nestled amongst a grove of pink and yellow trees, its door open, inviting. But inside, she was run by a cold and calculating artificial intelligence, driven mad by decades spent lost and alone amongst the stars. Sophie shuddered at the thought. "What does she wait for?"

"She waits for curious boys and girls. For naughty children to find her and climb aboard, then whoosh! She locks the doors and takes off." He paused, then looked her in the eye. "Never to be seen again."

Her uncle's words penetrated Sophie's heart with an icy dread. She exhaled another cloud of white fog as her eyes darted between the distant ship and her uncle, searching for the familiar joking glint in his eyes, the sly smile at the corner of his mouth.

He wasn't smiling.

Something was wrong.

Sophie forced a laugh. "They're never seen again, Uncle?" Her voice shook.

He glanced back at the distant ship and shook his head before reaching down and gripping her hand, burying her pale pink and white glove under the darkness of his.

Finding some courage deep within herself, Sophie clung to her uncle's hand as tight as she could. *It's just a story.* Her thoughts trickled back to the keeping safe classes at school. "I heard when kids disappear, it's more likely they're taken by someone they know." Her voice was a faint, choked whisper. "They never said anything about a hundred-year-old ship."

Robb's eyes were soft with sorrow, with guilt. He nodded, swallowed, and tried to smile. "It's always someone they know."

About the Author:

Austin P. Sheehan is a writer of speculative fiction and a lover of language, literature and '90s TV. Armed with a psychology degree, he went out into the world to further study humanity, and now prefers the company of his wife and greyhounds.

While living in Melbourne's inner suburbs, Austin wrote his debut novella Submerged City *(published by Deadset Press), but he has since moved closer to the mountains. You'll often find mountains in his stories, whether they are science fiction, fantasy, alternative history or horror.*

Find him on twitter @AustinPSheehan, go to www.austinpsheehan.com.

A Tale of Hearts and Horns

Nikky Lee

The frost is thick on the plains when the Hunter sets out. Coals from the campfire are long cold and he dons his cloak of goat hide, takes up his spear, and crunches over the icy grass. He walks into the sunrise, eyes searching, first the ground, then the horizon, hoping for a cloven imprint, a pile of dung or a four-legged silhouette outlined in the sun.

He sees nothing. But then, aurochs are not easy to find. The plains are vast—all he's ever known in his short life—running from the boggy marshes and Ur's towering ziggurats in the south to Sippar's wool dynasty in the north.

It's an impossible task he's been set, and he knows it, but proceeds anyway. Because it's for a girl. One he loves—or thinks he does.

Her price: an auroch. A bull for a bride. Her father will accept no less. A man (or a boy in his case) must prove his worth, that he can provide, said her father when he'd asked for her hand.

Of course, he could have gone to the village cow herder; asked Sumat for his best bull and presented it. But the village head wouldn't go trading his daughter for a mere cow. Aurochs are wild creatures, shoulders taller than the boy's head, girth wider than his reach, and with horns that could fit two of him between their tips. Such a prize could buy him a hundred brides across the plains, but he'll settle for just one. Each night he recalls her smooth cheeks, dark in the firelight, soft hair under his fingers, and a flash of white teeth as she leans in, shedding her day-mask of chaste village girl like a snakeskin.

"Wait for me, Ku-aya," he told her before he'd left.

Back in her mask, Ku-aya had not responded, not with her father watching, but just as the Hunter turned to leave, he'd caught the smile and ever-so-slight incline of her head.

So he hunts and hopes, day after day on the plains. His supplies—a water skin and three loaves of hard flatbread are tied in a sack at his waist—dwindling to a trickle and crumbs. If he does not find his prize soon, he'll have to return. Empty handed. The thought quickens his steps as he follows the Blue River, Id-Ugina, eyes scouring the bank for that elusive hoofprint. Each heartbeat he is disappointed. And in the fading dusk, when the skies open and the rain plummets, turning his boots sodden and extremities numb, the Hunter screams at the heavens, cursing the gods. First Enlil for sending the storm, then Utu for not shining longer.

He cannot get his fire started. The ground is wet, wood damp and the kindling green. His stomach rumbles and he throws down his tools, curses again, and wraps himself in his cloak to wait out the night. Only, he doesn't.

A bray, low and soft and almost lost in the patter of rain, reaches him.

The Hunter pauses, breath turning light in his chest, sure he imagined it. But there it is again. A hum on the edge of hearing, like the murmur of an incantation hymn, the kind En priests sing under their breath in the temples. A shiver passes over the Hunter; hairs prickling in the wet as he clutches his spear and trails the sound.

By the light of the moon, he picks his way along the bank. Pauses, listens, takes three steps then pauses again, until a shadow—a bovine head, black on black—shifts in the dim. It stands under a lone cedar tree, head turned windward. A snuff, and the Hunter goes rigid on the bank, imagining those nostrils twitching, catching his scent, and the twin horns lowering to charge. A heartbeat passes, then two. The auroch brays again, stamps once, then heads for the water. The twin horns lower and a gentle lapping reaches the Hunter's ears. Slowly, the Hunter lowers himself into the reeds, forcing stillness lest he startle the beast. His hands twitch around his spear, energy brimming under his skin. He hardly dares breathe. An auroch. An auroch here. For him.

Godsent, it must be.

A sign.

On the bank, the auroch shivers, the sheen of its black fur rippling like the waters of Id-Ugina before it, and the Hunter is transfixed, eyes lingering on the white fur stripe that runs down its muscled neck. Beautiful in its power.

He must have it. His family might be poor, his lands small, but Ku-aya's father can't ignore such an offer, or the status it would bring. The Hunter grins, imagining the look on her father's face when he leads the bull back into his village.

Ku-aya's hand is as good as his.

He uncoils the rope from his shoulder, forms a large loop at one end with a sliding knot. He considers the best approach. There's no way he can match the beast's strength. Its shoulder stands taller than he does. He squints at the long legs, far longer than any cow he's ever seen. Those are legs made for running. If it flees, there'll be no catching it.

Out from the reeds he slinks, creeping for the lone cedar further up the bank, holding his breath as he goes. The auroch, nose deep in the water, wallows forward, emitting another contented bray to the night. The Hunter ties one end of his rope around the cedar; tests the knot. It's a good rope, fresh and well made, but now its weave feels thin and flimsy in his sweaty palms. He pokes his spear into the slipknot at the rope's other end and holds it out at length.

With a quick prayer to the gods, he tiptoes down the bank, soundless, easing each foot into place before shifting his weight. So he goes. Ten paces out from the auroch, the beast snorts and shifts its bulk. Its ears twitch. The Hunter stops, caught mid step, sure he's been seen.

With a huff, the auroch shifts again and settles onto its knees in the water, jaw working as it chews its cud.

It's as if the gods are inviting him. Go on, he imagines Enlil calling on the breeze. Take it.

He steals forward; the rope loop dangling at the end of his spear quivers. One step, two. Easy does it. His feet sink into wet sand, cool moisture pricking between his toes. Closer. Closer. He reaches his spear and rope loop out, arching it over the auroch's head like a snake stretching its body from a tree and drops the loop over one horn, then yanks it tight.

The auroch starts, and with a bellow the Hunter feels in his chest, it leaps up from the water, thrashing and bucking, snapping its head this way and that. Eyes bulge in its head: a ring of white around dark irises.

Attached to the cedar tree, the rope snaps taut, pinging a note into the dark like the string of a lyre. The woven strands creak under the strain, and the Hunter braces for the inevitable pop of it tearing in two. But it never comes. The beast kicks; the white eel stripe down its back bunches and writhes. Water sprays the Hunter on the shore. Another bellow.

It happens too suddenly for the Hunter to react. The auroch jumps, twisting and bucking in the air; the rope catches under one hoof. In half a breath, the line is tangled in its legs, knotting around its knees and dragging its head down. Its nose dips the shallows. Muscles flex. The rope digs in, its grip somehow wrapped around the auroch's neck. The beast teeters, grace and beauty gone. Just a panicked animal on the plains.

Then it falls.

From the bank, the Hunter watches it all unfold. The auroch flails, hind hooves running at the air, its two horns the only part of its head above the waterline. Bubbles rise between them. Fast at first, then slower, and slower again. Part of The Hunter's mind is screaming, telling him to take up his knife and cut the rope. But it is a small part. The rest of him watches from a place outside himself, horror locking his muscles still, mind numb.

At last, the twitching stops.

Still the Hunter stands there, stunned. He counts the rush of his heart in his ears until he runs out of numbers he knows. Then his body is moving without him, finally sliding the knife free of its sheath and sawing through the rope. Water presses cold around his calves as he wades in, reaching for the horns.

A small shake. The head is so heavy it barely moves.

Nothing.

The Hunter's hand slips into the water and runs along the beast's neck. The fur is wet, still warm, but there's no throb of life underneath. Then his fingers meet rope, welted into a ridge in the animal's flesh and he recoils as if burned.

His stomach folds. Nausea rises in his throat. Inexplicable. He's seen death before. Killed before. This should be no different. Yet his hands shake, sweat stings his eyes. He'd not meant to kill it. One auroch eye meets his; the empty stare accusing, robbed of its lively gleam, and the wrongness of it twists the Hunter's stomach.

He stumbles back onto the bank, reaching it just as his stomach heaves.

The Hunter forces himself to rest. Rest and see what the morning brings. Perhaps then he can find a way to salvage the situation. The bull is not alive, but perhaps Ku-aya's father might accept a set of auroch horns for above his hearth, the Hunter thinks as he lies under the cedar, staring through its branches to the dark above, trying to ignore the disappointment lying heavy in his belly. If he stripped the carcass, it would feed Ku-aya's and her family for months—was that not providing? But how would he carry it all back with him? The Hunter rolls onto one side, then the other, unable to find comfort. Once he leaves the bull's body, he cannot return. River eels and scavengers will strip the carcass bare in a matter of days. The Hunter tears his hands through the black coils at his brow, stiff with grit and sweat from the plains, and closes his eyes.

A crackle in his ears snaps him awake. Two arm spans away, a fire burns, flames darting around a log set in a hollow of earth dug in the grass. On the other side, two eyes reflect the orange glow, their light dancing in time with the flames.

The Hunter gasps, comes to his knees, and scrabbles for his knife.

The eyes shift, the body behind moving into the light to reveal a face—dark skin, angular cheeks, square jaw. "My bull is dead."

For a moment the Hunter thinks it is a man, but then for a heartbeat, its features appear delicate, almost womanly, and the grey eyes drink him in.

They speak again. "Why did you kill him?"

The Hunter swallows, licks his lips, but his voice doesn't come. It's scurried somewhere down his larynx. The face shifts again, man, woman, man, features never quite settling. This is not the face of his kind. This is something else. At last, his words return. "Who are you?"

The being on the other side the fire cocks their head. Hairs prickle down the Hunter's neck. They look at him the same way a hawk might study the passage of a rat with passing interest, as if wondering whether or not to swoop. "Men call me Inanna."

The Hunter's blood curdles and his eyes turn nightward. The specks above are as cold and hard as the gaze across the fire. Inanna. God of the heavens. A croak rises in his throat before his voice flees again.

Full lips twitch in the shifting face, teeth flash. "You have heard of me then."

The Hunter falls to his knees, bows his head, prostrating himself in the grass. Heavens and stars. A god. And he'd just killed their bull. "I—" he begins, and stops. Something is wrong with his head. It feels heavy; awkward against the earth. His fingers go to his brow, smooth skin meets his touch, but when they travel left and right they each bump against a ridge of something smooth and hard. Something inside the Hunter squeezes, stealing his breath. His fingers trace the ridges up and out, following their steep curve from his head. Horns.

He lurches up with a cry, hands patting his face—nose, still a man's, chin, the same. His hands curl around his ears. They are long, fur soft. His hands travel down, following the softness. His neck is thick, shoulders hunched with the weight of his head. At his chest, he finds smooth skin again and the Hunter knows a moment of relief before he squints at his feet in the dark. Cloven hooves poke from under his *kanauke* skirt. A flash of movement, and the Hunter spots the tufted tail swish between his misshapen knees. He is full auroch from the waist down.

He screams. A bray rushes out his throat, choking into the night. "Please," he begs. "Turn me back."

Inanna's gaze is unsettling as they study him. "I cannot." In the flickering fire, their features shift and change like fish scales in the sun.

The Hunter tries again. "Please . . ." His chest itches, and he rubs it but can't shake the sense of emptiness underneath his ribs. "It was an accident. Please!"

Inanna lifts a hand, beckons with a finger. The Hunter stumbles forward, awkward and eager, but a hoof-step behind him stops him still. The auroch melts into the firelight, huge beside the Hunter, the muscles in its long legs twitching. And very much alive. It paces past him towards its owner, leaving no prints in its passing. The Hunter ogles at it.

"But I . . . what," he tries, falters, tries again. "How?"

Inanna strokes the bull's nose. "I used your heart."

Anger flares inside the Hunter, hot as a crafter's kiln. "You stole my heart?"

"You stole my bull."

The Hunter fights for composure; to not scream and wail at the heavens. After all, the God of Heaven is here, listening. He swallows, tasting earth on his tongue. "It was an accident." He forces himself to look into those iron eyes. "Please, I'll do anything."

A pause. "Anything?"

Something in the way Inanna says it prickles in the Hunter's chest, itches at his hollow. *Careful,* it warns. He ignores it. "Anything."

Inanna's smile broadens and they rise, a smooth motion, like water flowing upwards, their body a hymn of skin and corded muscle, power and beauty, man and woman. For a moment, the Hunter forgets himself and gapes, then feels a familiar stirring in his loins. He pries his gaze free and stares at the grass.

Ku-aya, think of Ku-aya!

Inanna's feet stop before him, toes curling in the stalks.

"Bring me a new heart." Inanna's voice issues from above. "And I'll swap it for yours." A finger under his chin tilts his head up and into those iron-studded eyes. The hollow inside him twists, an invisible hand clenching around the space that was. "A good heart, Hunter. Strong, full of life. Like for like. I'll accept nothing less."

The Hunter licks his lips. "And when I find it?"

"I will tell you the words to summon me."

Inanna whispers the sounds to him in the dark and makes him repeat them back.

"Good," they purr and return to the auroch's side. "Good luck, Hunter."

He wakes with a start. A dream. Thank the gods, just a dream. He lifts a hand to his head and his fingers knock against one of his horns. His howl sends a flock of larks into the sky.

Not a dream.

His eyes come to rest again on his cloven feet. Just one morning ago, he had toes. His stomach twists and he averts his gaze. He dares not look at his face in the waters of Id-Ugina, but he imagines what he might find there. A misshapen head; auroch's eyes staring out of his own. A sob catches in his throat and comes out as a soft bray on his breath.

A frantic quacking and a beat of wings from the reeds makes him start: a waterfowl taking flight. The Hunter curses, hugs himself, and tries not to stare at the fur on the back of his hands.

He cannot return like this. The village would turn him out. His family too. And Ku-aya . . . his stomach drops into that empty space inside him, like a stone down empty well. What would Ku-aya think?

A heart for a heart, Inanna had said. How hard could it be? His eyes track the waterfowl above. Too far away now to bring it down with a well-placed stone. Dazed, as if woken from a deep sleep, he gathers his things, hands going through the motions: coiling the rope back into tidy loops, bundling his last scrap of bread into the pouch on his belt and taking his waterskin down to the banks of Id-Ugina.

At the water's edge, where he will not look at his reflection, a soft hiss rises from the reeds. The Hunter stiffens, years of hunting on the plains and more years of stories as a child have attuned him to that sound. He remains still, eyes searching out the source. There. A flicker of a tongue, a glint of eyes watching from between the stalks. A water snake. The Hunter relaxes a little. Not the venomous cobra, or one of the many cantankerous vipers that strike first and ask questions later. No, this snake is smaller, perhaps the length of his arm and half again, hard to tell with it coiled among the reeds, skin a muddy green, eyes bright.

Full of life.

Might it be that simple? The Hunter hesitates.

Only one way to know.

He strikes fast, faster than he ever has before. His future rides on this. His fingers snap around its neck. The snake emits a muffled hiss before his hand clamps tight. The long body writhes, knotting over itself, around his wrist.

Crouched in the reeds, the Hunter's free hand combs Id-Ugina's shallows, curls around a rock in the water, pulls it up. He lifts the stone high over his head, then swings it down, bashing the snake's skull in. Mud and river silt splatter his chest. The reptile unknots in his grip. Cool blood drips down his palm.

The Hunter staggers to shore, flops to his knees. He lays the limp creature in the grass, pale belly up, and says the summoning words.

One beat passes. Then another.

A trickle of panic stirs in him. Perhaps he said the words wrong. Perhaps he has not presented his offering to Inanna's satisfaction. Quickly, he draws out his knife, slices the snake open, roots inside its miniature ribs like a mole hunting for worms. He plucks the heart free. So small. A pea in his palm. A plum in miniature.

Size doesn't matter. It's the life Inanna wants. He counsels and says the words again.

A breeze tickles the back of The Hunter's neck, stirring his fur on end. The pressure rises into a gust and shakes the leaves of the cedar, creaks the branches. For a moment he swears he hears, with his cursed auroch senses, a distant laugh.

But no god.

Try again, Hunter.

Any life, it seems, will not do.

He buries the snake, whispering an apology to it and Ningizida, God of Snakes and the Netherworld, as he turns the earth over the broken body. The smell of it follows him up the river as he walks, tasting copper on his tongue.

He kills a gazelle next. He downs it with a well-placed knife, thrown into the herd before they spooked and fled, leaving the injured doe behind. When he cuts it open he finds a fawn in the womb. He offers both hearts to Inanna, lying them side by side on the ground with bloody hands.

They don't come.

He waits for the breeze. But that doesn't come either. The evening is still; hot and sticky in the long light. Strange this, he wonders as he stares at the hearts, a few nights ago he'd been chafing his fingers together to keep them warm.

When he sleeps, he dreams of returning to Ku-aya, whole and a man once more. Together they sneak into the furthest field and lie in the barley, the golden stalks scratching their skin, tickling their thighs.

"What took you so long?" Ku-aya asks when they are done.

The Hunter opens his mouth to answer, but a bray comes out instead. *No, it can't be.* He is whole. He must be whole.

Ku-aya frowns, her eyes search his face, lingering on his head, his ears. She shifts in his arms, her weight pulling backwards. "What's happened to you?"

"It's nothing. It's still me," the Hunter says. He reaches for her. Black fur ropes his fingers. He snatches it away. But too late, she's already seen. Her eyes drop to his legs, spies his hooves, the tail poking out his *kaunake*. She sucks in a breath and worms out of his hold.

The Hunter scrambles after her. "It's alright, I'll find a heart," he says. He catches her wrist, pulls her in. "Ku-aya, please!"

She writhes. He catches her other hand, holds her still. "Please Ku-aya, it's me. It's still me!"

She bites him. Her teeth sink into his arm, driving deep. The Hunter yelps, pain sparking through him. He pulls away. Ku-aya stays still, eyes locked on his, confused and dazed. She coughs. Blood bubbles over her lips. Then her face slackens, the brightness dims in her eyes and they roll into her head.

The Hunter feels a familiar, horrifying warmth drip from his fingers. He looks down.

Ku-aya's heart is clenched in his grip.

His scream wakes him. Night greets his return. The fire has burnt low, the gazelle meat strung up like shadows above it. The Hunter gets two breaths in before his stomach turns and he retches. Gazelle meat and river water slop onto the grass. Shaking, he slumps back and curls into himself, waiting for his breath to slow, the tightness in his hollow chest to ease. Ku-aya's last expression comes to him. So shocked and betrayed, her gaze reaching at him, wondering what she did to deserve this.

Is that what you want, Inanna?

Cold dread radiates from his gut, spreading through his limbs like venom. *Not her. Please, Inanna.*

The cold presses in, sits on his chest and makes it hard to breathe. *Anyone but her.*

As if in answer, the breeze shifts, buffeting the coals and setting the smoked meat swinging.

The cold in his gut vanishes, hot adrenaline taking its place as a new smell reaches him. He rocks to his hooves, quivering, ears twitching in the dark.

And then he hears the voices.

Words rise out of the night.

"Abba, someone's out there." The voice is light and unbroken. A boy's. The Hunter can't make him out yet, but he imagines a finger rising and pointing at his smouldering fire. Imagines the horror creep over a young, beardless face at the sight of him.

No! Don't look. He stumbles back.

"They moved!" The boy says. "Abba, it's a man."

The Hunter feels for his satchel, then his knife. His hand shakes, fingers sweaty on the hilt. *Please, just go away.*

"I see him." The second voice is older, husky from use. It clears phlegm from its throat, then calls: "You, by the fire, what are you doing so far from the Ur road?"

The Ur road? He'd come further south than he'd thought. The Hunter blinks into the night, willing his eyes to focus. Bit by bit, he makes out two figures, one shorter than the other and barely twelve kush away. He can't make out their faces, but he reads the apprehension in the taller figure's frame—something in the stiffness of the shoulders.

A waft of livestock meets his nose, then a faint moo. Cows. Behind the figures, a herd of shadows move. The Hunter's breath catches. Could he . . ? No, Inanna would never accept a cow, no matter how strong or lively. The god has made their wish clear. But what if he offered a *dozen* cows? Could it be enough? Enough to spare Ku-aya?

For Ku-aya, I'll slaughter a hundred.

The wind tickles his ears, ruffles the hair around his horns. Almost as if it approves.

"Sir? Are you lost?"

The Hunter's mind races. A dozen cows. He could do it. Open their jugulars, bleed them on the bank of Id-Ugina, then present their hearts to Inanna on the dawn. But there was the matter of the cowherd and his brood . . . how to deal with them?

The cowherd is still talking: "The road to Ur is three uš east of here, off the—"

"Abba!" the boy hisses; he's come closer in the dark. They both have.

They stiffen, some intrinsic sense that warns of danger; the Hunter has it too. Or had it. Briefly, he wonders when that changed. No matter. He shifts his weight, his trembling body stilling.

"Now there, stranger," the taller one begins. "Let's not have any trouble. We'll water the cattle then leave you in peace." One arm reaches out, placating. Away from the fire, the Hunter finally makes out his face, it's thin with a trim beard and crowded teeth hang inside his gaping mouth. The boy beside him is thin too, gangly from growing, and he's staring.

"Abba, it's not a man," he says.

A croak rises from the cowherd. He falls to his knees, pulls his kin down beside him and prostrates himself in the grass. "Forgive us, O'Maskim." *Forgive us, demon.* The Hunter's ears twitch at the word, his stomach tightens. *For Ku-aya.*

"Careful, Abba, there's no trusting them," the boy whispers to his father.

The cowherd cuffs him. "Be silent." And pushes his son's head harder into the earth. "Forgive him, he's not yet learned to weigh his words before speaking."

They've seen. By En and Enlil, they've seen. The Hunter pushes the panic down. He stamps one hoof into the ground beside the man's head, swats his tail. *Let them see.* He weighs his own words carefully, opens his mouth—

"Whatever I can offer in recompense, I'll gladly give," the cowherd blurts, lifting his head.

The Hunter meets his eye, steels his glare, thinking of Inanna's iron gaze. "Your herd."

"My . . . herd?" the cowherd gapes and the Hunter swings his horned head closer. The man swallows. "All of them?"

"All."

The cowherd stares aghast, like he might argue. He glances up at the horns again, then down to the cloven hooves. His mouth clicks shut. "Please accept our offering, O'Maskim." He bows low into the dirt.

The Hunter nods. "Blessing upon you." Unsure how to conclude the encounter, he brushes a hand over their heads. It feels right, somehow. Their hair tingles under his fingers; charged, like the air before a storm.

He tries not to think about it as the pair turn and flee into night.

Twelve cows. Twelve steaming carcasses. Twelve hearts piled before his fire. And Inanna, at last. A wry smile quirks the god's top lip as they survey the corpses. "This is quite the mess you've made."

"You came," the Hunter says, he tries to clean the dry blood crusted onto the back of his hands. "Is it enough?"

Inanna chuckles, voice turning into a two-toned harmony, like two strings of a lyre plucked at once; one note deep, the other high and tittering. "Skies no," they say.

The Hunter throws his knife down to the dirt, bites back a curse that could land him in even worse straits. "How many?" he demands. "How much more?"

Inanna grins. "Just the one heart, dear Hunter."

Just *one*? They couldn't mean . . . The slow, cold dread slithers back into the Hunter's belly, chilling him to the bone. His breath shudders. "No."

"No?" the god arches a thick brow; orange twilight glints off bronze cheekbones and strong, bare shoulders, but the iron eyes remain cold.

The Hunter gathers his courage and straightens his back. "No. I won't kill Ku-aya."

Inanna's lips press together. "Then a demon you'll remain. They're already hunting you, you know."

The Hunter shifts, hooves sucking into the blood-churned earth. "Who?"

"A cowherd and his boy arrived in Ur at noon today telling a tale of a maskim on the banks of Id-Ugina. A maskim who took their herd but gave them a blessing. I believe the cowherd later won big in Ur's gambling houses."

The Hunter blinks, ears pricking. "He did?" All he'd done was brush a hand to the man's head.

"Indeed." Inanna's wry smile returns, this time with teeth. They lean close to the Hunter's ear, breath tickling his fur, and produce a bronze coin in front of his eyes. A sheaf of wheat glosses one side. "He was murdered for three shekels."

Cold seeps up from the Hunters gut and around his chest. A shiver passes down his legs; his bovine tail gives a nervous flick. *What did I do?* The coin vanishes back into Inanna's *kaunake* wrap and they step away. Their head turns skyward, and for a beat the god's eyes soften to silver.

"Go home, Hunter. See your lover. Claim her heart, before there's nothing left to claim."

He stiffens. "What do you mean?"

"Go home," Inanna says again.

Fear constricts his throat. The Hunter swallows and forces the words out. "Is Ku-aya sick?" He snatches his satchel from the fireside and starts stuffing his supplies into it. "Well?" he demands, wariness forgotten. When the god doesn't answer, he pauses, looks up.

Inanna is gone. He is talking to an empty night.

It is dark again when he returns to his village, sulking from shadow to shadow, trying his best to hide his form as he makes his way through the barley fields. Drumbeats thrum the air and the sound pulses in the hollow of his chest. They're celebrating. As he draws closer to the buildings, he picks out more instruments: flute; lyre; *voices*. Not just any old strangers. There, that's Sumat's drunken bellow, Nirah the basket weaver's smooth notes—he listens for one voice in particular, but can't hear her.

Fear puts a spoon to his gut and churns and he hurries up to the first of the mud-brick homes, peering around its wall into the trading square. Feasting tables line the centre of the square, piled with fruit, breads, and cooked meats. A wedding feast. Villagers mill in clumps of two and three, talking and laughing as they sip cloudy *sikar* through reed straws. A whiff of the fermented barley brew reaches the Hunter and he licks his lips, longing for a taste. He stamps down on the desire.

Ku-aya first.

He searches the crowd, eyes darting from group to group, half expecting to see her figure squatting among the children, whispering mischief into their ears. But not this time. The Hunter eyes a group of unmarried girls, wondering if her sharp tongue has got her sent home; it wouldn't be the first time.

When a child runs past, his *kaunake* skirt cradling a mound of dates from the table, the Hunter ducks back behind the wall, the hollow inside him spasming. Not sure whether the thought of being seen or being recognised scares him more, the Hunter swallows, rubs his sweaty hands on his kaunake and, when he's sure the child is long gone, peeks out—

And spots the newlyweds at the head of the square. Something in the bride's posture is off; her back is straight, chin high, shoulders stiff in the same way Ku-aya's goes when she speaks about her father—a rare thing, but not unheard of.

"Let's not talk about him," she'd spat the last time, flicking her hair out of her face with a disdainful finger. *"All he cares about is selling me off to a wealthy husband."*

In the square, the bride lifts her hand and flicks a stray lock aside.

The Hunter stares, horror building inside him like a scream. Ku-aya. It's *Ku-aya.*

Beside her, a man lounges in the cushions, talking animatedly to a wool trader from Kish. His head is shaved smooth, eyes alight, and there's no mistaking the grin on the groom's face, even from a distance.

The Hunter eyes the groom's coiled beard in envy, fingers brushing the feathery bristles on his own chin as he searches his memory for the man's name. He's a wool trader too, out-of-town, but rich; Ku-aya's father had introduced them once in the market—before the Hunter had asked for Ku-aya's hand. Sin . . . Sin-nagar? No, Sin-nasir. The merchant talking to him moves off, and Sin-nasir turns to Ku-aya, gesturing at the figs on the table. His gaze lingers on her lips, then the golden leaves of her headdress, and the Hunter catches the raised notes of a question. Ku-aya shakes her head. The groom slumps a little, puts the fig down, his lips drawn tight, as if he'd just taken a mouthful of sour wine. His eyes slide to Ku-aya, inspecting her figure through her kaunake. She senses it and stiffens.

Why are you just sitting there? The Hunter wants to shout at her. This isn't the Ku-aya he knew. Ku-aya did what she wanted, when she wanted. The Hunter fights down panic, and then the urge to charge into the celebration, knock the tables asunder.

What if she does *want this?* The fresh thought bites into him. *No, she mustn't. Look at her up there.*

A scream pierces the gathering. Shrill. Blood-chilling. And *close.*

The Hunter spins and finds the child—the one who'd been stealing dates from the tables, named Ak something, Akim?—standing at the Hunter's back, a pool of urine darkening the earth under him. His mouth is open, eyes snared on the Hunter, colour draining from his face. He screams like he's seen one of his nightmares come to life. Maybe he has.

Silence smothers the celebration. Heads turn, seeking the source of the noise. The Hunter staggers away, plunging back down the dark road. He startles an elderly couple heading back early to their mud-brick home.

They scream. The man faints. And the woman's shouts hound him into the night. "Monster! Maskim! Be gone!"

And the Hunter flees, crashing through the village fields, flattening crops under his hooves until the sounds of the village fade. At the banks of Id-Ugina he falls to his knees, the hollow inside him aching, and tears at his horns as if hoping to rip them out of his head. His fingers dig into the fur at his shoulders, like he might peel it off—just as he does when stripping the hide of a kill. But all he does is draw blood.

When he screams, it comes out as a long, piercing bray.

Not even the wind responds.

It is past midnight before the Hunter dares to sneak back—against his better judgment. *She's married now, there's nothing you can do. Ku-aya's heart belongs to Sin-nasir.* But still his hooves carry him across the fields, heading home, heading to Ku-aya. *One last goodbye,* he tells himself. A last goodbye before he goes west into the desert and dooms himself to monsterhood; to do whatever it is maskim do.

Normally, a groom would take his bride back to his own household, but Sin-nasir has no home here. There is only one place they will be.

The Hunter steals back into the streets, wincing at the soft thud-thud of his hooves and tries to time his steps to the wedding drums. He finds the house easily; he knows the way by heart—or by whatever beats inside him. The square, flat-roofed silhouette throws a familiar shadow over the open courtyard of Ku-aya's family home. All the windows are dark, bar one above the open doorway into the courtyard; everyone has vacated into the homes of friends and extended family while Sin-nasir is in town.

The Hunter sinks into the shadows and listens. No sounds, but the faint hiss of a fire in an oil lamp. Certain the newlyweds are not inside, he approaches, stretches to his full height and places a white poppy on the windowsill—as he always had. When last he'd left this message, Ku-aya had found him waiting in the street outside and they'd snuck into the fields to eat the poppy seeds together. He slinks back to the edge of the courtyard. All he can do now is hope she sees it.

The moon is full and low in the sky when the drums and music stop. Roused by the silence, the Hunter makes sure his form is hidden in the shadow of the wall and waits. Sure enough, footsteps approach the front of the house. One set is heavy, scuffing on the dirt, the other is faint, light on the ground and delicate, each step carefully placed to make minimal sound. The ache in the Hunter's chest squeezes around his ribs: he'd taught her that. *Like a plains cat on the prowl,* he'd once instructed and marvelled at how quickly she'd picked it up.

In the window, the lamp light flickers as figures cross the room.

"Come to bed, my love." Sin-nasir's quiet urging drifts down to the courtyard.

Ku-aya laughs. "Why the rush, dear husband? We have all night." Her words lance a tendril of fear into the Hunter's gut. *Could she really want this?* Her figure appears at the window, hands find the dead flower. It's too dark to make out her expression; the light of the lamp shadows her face.

The Hunter fights an exasperated groan and forces himself still. Wait. Patience.

Then Sin-nasir's arms wrap around her and he nuzzles into her neck. "Come to bed," he whispers, drawing her back. For a beat, the light catches Ku-aya's face. It's wooden; the forced smile she wears for her father. She turns on him, fingers wandering up his chest.

"I'm afraid I've drunk far too much sikar," she says. "I need a chamber pot."

The Hunter holds his breath, ears rammed up at the window. Blood rushes in his head. She saw the poppy. She's coming.

Sin-nasir sighs as Ku-aya pulls away from him. "Be quick."

Ku-aya tut-tuts him and pads from the room. The Hunter quivers and swallows, tongue suddenly thick in his mouth. Her feet, barely audible, whisk closer. He anxiously pats his horns, as if trying to smooth them back like errant curls. They stay rigid on his head and he recoils into the dark, stomach writhing. Her silhouette arrives at the door, then steps out. The Hunter struggles for breath, labouring for the right words as she hurries across the courtyard, heading for the street. *Call her name,* he commands his voice, but it doesn't obey. Fear pumps in his ears. *Call her name!* he wills again.

But she'll see, Fear answers, freezing him in place. Fists clench as he batters it down. *CALL HER.*

"Ku-aya!" It comes out as a grunt.

At the street's edge, she pauses, steps back and squints into the dark. "Who's there?"

The Hunter clears his throat. "It's me."

Ku-aya's head snaps around, moonlight catching her as hope and uncertainty clash across her face. "You," her voice shakes. She swallows and straightens. "Where have you been? You've been gone for months!"

Months? That's not possible. The Hunter counts the days as far as he is able. Even so, he's sure he's not mistaken. "It's only been a few weeks."

"It's been four months, you swine!" Ku-aya hisses. She takes a blind step towards him in the dark and the Hunter dances back, grimacing at the clump of his hooves on the dirt. Ku-aya's eyes latch onto his shadow and her anger softens. "I thought you were dead. I thought my father's ridiculous request for a bull got you killed. I even wondered whether he might have had a part in it. En and Enlil, he was insufferable when you didn't come back." She huffs, hands going to her hips, but it doesn't disguise the tremor in her arms. "But you're here now, that's what matters. It's not too late." She reaches for him.

"P-Please." The Hunter throws out a hand to ward her away. "Stay there."

Ku-aya frowns, gaze drawn to his fingers and his black, auroch-furred hand. He snatches it back. Her frown deepens into a scowl. "What are you hiding?" She presses in.

"Don't," he stammers. Quick as a viper, her fingers catch his wrist and she reels herself in until they're chest to chest. Gods, her smell, sweet cedar and cypress. He sways, the oil in her hair wicking up his nose, into his lungs and igniting the ache in his crotch. Her hands find his face, cup his cheeks. She leans in—

And stops.

The Hunter's ears twitch as she snatches a breath. Her eyes, pupils wide and black in the dark, travel up, along his horns, then down to his bovine legs. He expects her to scream, or maybe prostrate herself like the cowherd did and beg forgiveness. Ku-aya does neither. She studies him.

From the window, a snore cuts short. Muttering, then Sin-nasir's groggy coos reach them: "Where have you gone, my dearest?"

Ku-aya's grip tightens around the Hunter's arms. Rage flashes across her face before she relaxes again. "Just a little longer, husband," she calls. "Lady's business."

A grumble responds, but a beat later, another snore rises over the sill.

Ku-aya pulls the Hunter to the edge of the courtyard. "En and Enlil, what happened?" she whispers.

He doesn't know where to begin. The story comes out in a jumble. Inanna, the auroch, something about a snake, the cowherd and his boy, his search for a heart, Inanna's demand it be hers. Ku-aya listens, saying nothing until he runs out of words.

"A heart, you say?" she says when he is done. She sits beside him on the wall, fingers lacing with his. She strokes the back of his hand, sending a tingle down his arm.

The Hunter nods, stomach knotting. He shouldn't have come here. Not on her wedding night.

"Well, I can't go giving you mine," Ku-aya reasons. She puzzles a moment, dark brows knitting before her eyes snap to his. "You love me, don't you?"

"Always."

She smiles; a secret smile, one she uses when she knows something he doesn't. "Then wait here."

Ku-aya detaches herself from him, the air turning cool at the Hunter's side as she crosses the courtyard and over the threshold of her home. The Hunter starts after her; she shoots him a warning glance. He stills. "I won't be long," she says.

For a beat the dark drinks her in, then she is gone. He strains his ears, for what he's not sure. His tail gives a nervous swish under his *kanauke*. How far away is dawn? He can't stay much longer. *Shouldn't* stay. This is a far longer goodbye than—

A shout rips from the window: male, loud. Sin-nasir. The Hunter freezes. She's been discovered. There's a grunt, the sounds of two bodies struggling. Then a squeal, like a hen's screech under an axe. Something heavy thuds to the floor. Gasping. Gurgling.

"Ku-aya!" The Hunter is on his feet, blundering through the doorway before he can think. The room is dark, his horns catch on something hanging from the ceiling. Herbs. He thrashes through, scattering dried leaves. Up the stairs. Hooves clatter, slip-sliding for purchase. "Ku-aya!" He barrels into the room.

She's hunched over Sin-nasir. One glance and the Hunter knows he's dead. Blood pools under the body, thick and steaming; it cloys up the Hunter's nose as he draws close. A grinding, grating sound emanates from Ku-aya. Cold spreads down the Hunter's throat, clutching at his hollow. He takes a step, then two, until he can see her fully.

Straddled over her husband, she saws at his exposed ribs with a bronze kitchen knife. A rib cracks, followed by the pop of another and she pulls his rib cage open like a bloody flower.

The Hunter stares, transfixed, unable to move, not even look away.

Ku-aya's hand slides between the bones, her knife flashing deep. Once, twice, half a dozen times. Then she pulls, slowly, bit by careful bit and draws out Sin-nasir's heart. The Hunter chokes down a cry, like it's his heart she's ripping out. Ku-aya, his dear, clever, mischievous Ku-aya. *Why?*

"You've been going about it all wrong," she says, and a smile crooks her lips.

The Hunter tastes copper in the air. Her sweet cedar and cypress scent is gone. His hollow aches; he fights down tears. ". . . I have?"

Ku-aya paces towards him. Heart cupped in her palms as if presenting a gift. "You've been trying to retrieve your old heart," she says, and he tries not to look at the red flecks on her cheeks. "But instead, you just need to take a new one."

The Hunter quivers. "But my heart—"

Her expression hardens. "Is gone. It's in Inanna's hands now."

"But they said—"

"Gods and their games," she spits. "Do you think you'll really get it back?"

Not unless I trade it for yours. The words whisper through his thoughts, rising the hairs on his neck before he shoves them down. *Never.* Not to Ku-aya. Not even now.

"Did Inanna say you couldn't replace your heart with another's?"

The Hunter thinks back, shakes his head.

Ku-aya pushes Sin-nasir's heart at him, red dribbling down her fingers. "Then take it."

Still he hesitates.

"Do you want to be whole or not?" she asks. "Do you want to be a man again?"

He nods and she places the heart in his hands. It's still warm. He stares at it. His lover's heart or this. Either way, he becomes a monster—this time for real. His eyes find Ku-aya standing opposite in the dark, red ugliness soaking her front. The hollow wrenches in his chest, like a pet monkey banging at the bars of its cage. He can't leave her. The village will kill her for this—and she knows it. He closes his eyes and holds back a sob. "What do I do?"

"Eat it."

He bites it like an apple; forcing his flat teeth through the muscle, tearing a chunk free. It's chewy, with a slightly gamey taste. He tries to swallow quickly, get it over with, but chokes and nearly vomits before he gets it down.

Something at the back of his mind is screaming. Sweat beads at his forehead.

The next bite is easier. He goes slower, it's easier to chew; his teeth are sharper. By the third bite, his skin itches; his legs feel oddly hot. He doesn't look. Bite, chew, swallow. And again. His belly fills, nausea rising inside him.

"Keep going," Ku-aya urges. "It's working."

At the last bite, his gut is squirming. He's so full he can hardly breathe. His chest is heavy, head light; sweat slicks his neck. One gulp and the last lump slides down his throat. He's panting, hands shaking. And feels a heart thud in his chest for the first time in weeks.

He turns his hands over. Smooth skin. He feels for his horns, only to find gritty curls instead. A glance at his feet as he almost swoons. Toes. He has toes!

"Ku-aya, it worked!"

"I know, I see it!"

A slow clap sounds from the window.

They spin, Inanna sits on the sill, long legs crossed under the god like one of the great cats—apex predator of the plains.

"Well played, Hunter." They rise and circle Ku-aya, one moment chest bare and proud as an Ur warrior, the next all sultry curves—and then both at once.

It disturbs the Hunter, and he wrestles with it. But then, what does it matter? He was a man *and* an auroch, and Inanna is a god. An entity of the stars. Male, female; human, monster: these things are trivial to them.

Inanna pads to a stop before Ku-aya. "I see why he likes you." They grin, but their iron eyes are as distant as the Heaven they come from.

Ku-aya's bloody fingers clench into fists. "He's cured now. You have no hold over him," she says. If the Hunter didn't know her so well, he might not have noticed the quiver in her voice.

Inanna chuckles. "I'll give you this one, little snake."

Ku-aya blinks, even more uncertain. "Just like that?"

"It is not every day you surprise a god." Their gaze drops to Sin-nasir, dead on the floor. "Best not linger long," Inanna warns and turns for the window, muscles flexing as if they might spread their arms and take flight. "My thanks for the entertainment."

The pair walk into the dawn, putting the village behind them. They carry little; he can hunt what they need on the plains. She carries a small sack of supplies and stolen jewellery to sell once they reach Ur. It should buy them passage across the sea. Passage to a place where no one knows them or has heard of a god named Inanna.

Behind, their shadows stretch across the fields as they walk. And when they reach the river, one shadow, then the other, twitches, as if each throwing off a cloak. The shadows reach for one another, darkness tangling; limbs contorting into a single mass. Their owners walk on, oblivious, and in their wake, the darkness writhes. Its shoulders hunch, legs deform. The last thing to change is its head: it elongates and grows a set of horns.

About the Author:

Nikky grew up as a barefoot 90s child in Perth, Western Australia, before moving to New Zealand in 2016. By day she works as a professional content writer and by night authors speculative fiction, often burning the candle at both ends to explore fantastic worlds, mine asteroids and meet wizards. Her creative work has appeared in magazines, on radio and in anthologies around the world. She is currently writing a dark fantasy trilogy, routinely sacrificing literary darlings to the editing gods in the hopes of seeing it published.

You can find her online at:
W:nikkythewriter.com | T:@NikkyMLee | F:nikkythewriter

Tercio de Muerte

BG Hilton

The bull was old. That was obvious. Old, mangy, flyblown, barely standing. But it was standing, and it was blocking the tiny alley outside Carlos' cervezeria.

"Do you remember me, Carlos?" the bull said. Its voice was rough, raspy, cracked.

"I knew lots of bulls back in the day," Carlos said. He was not young himself, grey haired and heavy jowled. "You will have to refresh my memory, señor."

The bull looked with rheumy eyes past Carlos and towards a row of neat framed photographs behind the bar. They showed Carlos as a younger man—slender and handsome—posing in the bullring. Though the photos colours were faded, the bull could still make out the matador's gaudy traje de luces, as well as his montera and estoque. The real hat and sword were fastened above the bar, too, above the top shelf of bottles.

"No, señor," the bull said. "You pretend not to know me, but I see in your eyes you remember."

Carlos rubbed the side of his abdomen, just below his ribcage. "Ah, yes. Now I know you—though I do not recall you talking before.

In truth, now is not a good time to talk. It is the lunch rush, you see, and my customers will want a drink and some tapas, and you are blocking the alley."

The bull sniffed with disgust. "Why do so many retired matadors open bars?"

"Tradition, I expect," Carlos said.

"That is why you fight bulls, too?" the bull said. "Tradition?"

"But I do not fight bulls," Carlos said. "I am retired."

"You nearly missed your retirement," the bull said. "I nearly killed you."

"Nearly."

"An inch to the right, and they never would have sewn you up in time."

"And had I not appealed for your indulto—your pardon—you would have died too." Carlos looked past the bull, perhaps hoping to see customers. Seeing none, he sighed and poured himself a vino tinto. "So that is old times discussed," he continued, "and my life discussed. Now, what have you been up to? Ah, but I know the answer to that. You have been put out to stud, you lucky fellow. A retired fighting bull has the opposite fate to a retired matador. For us, the girls lose interest the minute we take off the montera."

"Yes, I was out to stud," the bull said. "But on my bull ranch, selective breeding was the least of the owner's interests. He had other ideas for improving the stock of fighting bulls. Genetic manipulation, surgery, cybernetics . . . He had some very strange notions."

"Had?"

"He is dead," the bull said, sketching the sign of the cross with its horns. "A new experiment . . . it kicked him to death. A pity. I'd no grudge against the fellow, mad as he was. He gave me a voice, and I enjoy talking."

"So I have observed," Carlos sighed. "Bull, what is your business with me? Granted ours was a fateful meeting, but have we not moved beyond it? I've no grudge over the gash in my side, though it aches in winter. And if you are still angry . . ."

"I am not angry," the bull said. "Merely thorough. In my life, I have done much. There is only one task that I began but did not finish. Perhaps, señor, the same is true of you?"

Carlos sighed. With an old man's care, he climbed onto a stool and took the montera and estoque down from their hooks. "Very well," he said. "Let us be thorough."

The bull pawed the ground and waited.

About the Author:

BG Hilton studied English at the University of Sydney; Writing at UTS, and writes when he's not wrangling his toddler. He blogs about Frankenstein movies, the Leonard Nimoy TV series In Search Of . . . *(aka Great Mysteries of the World) and also writes a free series of rambling soap-operatic spec-fic web stories at bghilton.com.*
You can also find him on Twitter @bghilton.

His short stories have been published in several venues, including Andromeda Spaceways, Antipodean SF, Pseudopod *and in the* Aries *volume of the zodiac series. His first novel, a Steampunk adventure story titled* Champagne Charlie and the Amazing Gladys *will be coming out from Odyssey Books in the near future. He lives in Sydney, but don't hold that against him.*

The Eternal Twilight of His Maze

Jenny Blackford

Ariadne's half-brother Asterion bellowed again and again from the labyrinth under King Minos' palace.

"Can't someone make him stop?" she shouted at the slaves clustered around her. "I can't stand it anymore!" She kicked out at her little table, cedar inlaid with ivory griffins, and priceless pots of cosmetics rolled over the painted floor.

Ariadne's old nurse Theodora ran in through the doorway and waved the other slaves out of the bedroom. "Calm, calm, princess," the old slave said, holding Ariadne's arm. "I have taken the Sacred One a sleeping draught. Goddess willing, he will not trouble you again tonight. And here, for you, a cup of honey wine. Sit down on your bed and drink it, sweetheart."

"Oh, all right," Ariadne said. "But he'd better keep quiet from now on."

She drained the silver cup, pretending not to notice the poppy juice mixed in with the sweet wine, and let Theodora lift her onto the gilded bed.

"Sleep now, sweetheart," her old nurse said, taking the cup from her.

Ariadne watched as Theodora righted the inlaid table and picked up the cosmetics in their finely-worked pots of gold and alabaster, placing them back in careful order. Finally, Theodora went to her pallet on the floor at the foot of the bed and lay down.

Ariadne stared at the blue and green dolphins on the ceiling for as long as she could, listening for any more bellowing from the Minotaur down in his labyrinth. If her half-brother let out another noise . . . But all she heard was old Theodora snoring softly. Soon, the poppy resin overcame her will, and she slept. Bulls trampled and bellowed through her dreams.

Long after dawn, she woke to the quiet noises of her slaves readying her most regal outfit, heavy with birds and flowers wrought in gold.

"I don't feel like doing anything much today," she told Theodora, who held the tray full of fruit and sweet wine for her breakfast. "Just cancel whatever's organized for me, will you? Maybe we could talk to the palace seamstresses. I've got some ideas."

Deep creases crossed on Theodora's wrinkled forehead. "We need to dress you up properly now and paint your face, sweetheart. Here, eat these lovely ripe figs, there's a good girl."

Ariadne threw two of the figs hard against the far wall. They splattered against the fresco: blue monkeys scampering up palm trees. "I don't *want* to," she said. "I won't."

Theodora swallowed. "The ship from Athens arrived at dawn, princess, bearing this year's tribute. You must go with your parents to receive them. Your father commands it. And tomorrow–well, you know what we must do tomorrow, together with the Sacred One. You and he are the ones chosen by the Goddess."

Ariadne took the crystal cup of wine from the tray and drained it. "Get me more wine. And some honey-cakes." She tipped the tray of fruit over the inlaid marble floor.

Down on her hands and knees gathering up the fruit, Theodora said, "Do not hate your brother, princess. Asterion is sacred to the Goddess, the Mistress of Animals. Of all creatures She made, the bull is the dearest to Her."

Ariadne couldn't bear to think about it. She didn't *hate* Asterion. He'd always been so sweet to her; he would do anything she asked him to. When he was sad, she could feel it in the pit of her stomach, even from the safe distance of her down-stuffed bed. But when he bellowed like that, it reminded everyone at the court that her half-brother was, well, half-bull. They all knew what her mother the Queen had done with that bull. It was so *embarrassing*.

She hated to think of her love-sick mother out in the fields twenty-two years ago, waiting inside that hide-covered cow-shaped wooden monstrosity, tempting Poseidon's beautiful bull to bestiality. Even that wasn't really her mother's fault. If her father, King Minos, hadn't . . . It was all too complicated, like anything to do with the gods. But Theodora was the only one who dared to mention her half-brother to her. In time, the old woman would die, and everyone else would forget all about him.

In the labyrinth under the palace, Asterion waited. Tomorrow, he would see his half-sister Ariadne, his mother's loveliest child. Her father was King Minos; his, the bull from the sea.

When the girl was younger, the royal nurse Theodora had brought her down to the labyrinth almost every day. "You two are chosen by the Goddess," she would say. "We should not question Her ways." The girl had been the one bright spot in the eternal twilight of his underground maze. His bull's mouth and throat were not made for human words, but they had played together as all children play, running and jumping and squealing through every corridor of this maze, his prison.

But when Ariadne's breasts had begun to swell, the visits had stopped. King Minos, with the authority of his father Zeus, had forbidden Theodora to bring the girl to the labyrinth. Now the old slave, who came each day to bring Asterion some barley cakes, soft cheese and wine, was his only visitor—except for the yearly sacrifice to the Goddess, the one secret, sacred duty that his half-sister shared with him. Soon, she would come, and they would make the ancient sacrifice on the altar at the heart of Daidalos' maze, with old Theodora as acolyte. It would be good, but it would be over all too soon. He missed his sister so much.

Asterion could *feel* his half-sister moving from room to room above him, eating and drinking and sleeping, sometimes dancing for the Goddess. He heard her voice always, almost heard her thoughts. She was too old now to play at chasing him through the winding corridors of his prison, or to throw golden balls for him to catch. But he would have given anything for just a few moments alone with her. Would he ever rest his hairy head on her lap again? When she was young, she used to stroke his wide nose, and pull at his soft furry ears, and giggle.

He could escape, if he wanted to—he knew the ways of the labyrinth as well as old artificer Daidalos, who'd designed it for him—but where would he go? The labyrinth was a safe haven, as well as a prison. There would be no life for him out in the open air, not these days. He was a throwback to the old times: a monster.

In the old days, he would have been worshipped, not imprisoned. If Ariadne had wished, they could have ruled the holy island of Crete together, with the blessing of the Goddess. But everything had changed, when sky-god Zeus had landed here with King Minos' mother Europa on his back. Only a few old slaves like Theodora remembered the old ways, now.

Ariadne stood with her sisters in the Great Room, each resplendently arrayed as a princess of the royal house of Minos. Her eyes were darkened, her face whitened, her lips reddened, and her hair curled. Above the short-sleeved cloth-of-gold bodice that the slaves had wrapped tightly around her waist, her lovely breasts were covered only with gauze. Her long purple skirt fell flounce over pleated flounce from her tiny waist to the marble floor, and beads of amber as big as cow's eyes circled her throat and arms. Moon-shaped rings of gold were heavy in her earlobes. She didn't want to be there, but she tried not to pout; it was so unattractive. She knew that she was more beautiful than anyone else in the room, but the frescoes all around her—girls and boys leaping lightly over the backs of gigantic bulls—niggled at her.

She could *feel* half-human Asterion down under the palace, alone in his twilight world, waiting.

Ariadne's father Minos, Lord of Knossos, was toying with the terrified group of Athenians that stood before him. On and on he droned about the death of his dear son, shamefully killed by the Athenian king after he'd won every contest in the Athenian Games. But what was the point? Tomorrow, all of the Athenians would be taken to the labyrinth below the palace, and none would return. Ariadne caught herself slumping with boredom and pulled herself up into perfect, regal posture.

"As recompense for my son's untimely death," Minos droned on, "we exact tribute from Athens. Seven young men and seven young women are chosen by lot every year, and carried here by ship, to be thrown to the savage Minotaur. This year, you are that tribute."

But what did her father seriously expect Asterion to *do* with the Athenians, once he sent them down to the labyrinth? *Eat* them? Surely he knew that bulls ate grass and barley. Her fool of a father had no idea of the sacrifice that Ariadne and her half-brother made each year, at the altar at the heart of the maze.

At last, the king finished his speech: "Do not blame us for your fate; blame the treachery of King Aegeus of Athens."

The Athenians had been just a huddled mass of undifferentiated prisoners to Ariadne, but one of them flinched when Minos spoke Aegeus' name. The princess watched the young man as he stood straighter, squared his wide shoulders and stared defiantly at the king. Suddenly, Ariadne's heart was racing, and her blood rang in her ears. How could she have failed to notice him? Her mouth was dry, and her skin burned.

He was *beautiful*. Was he a god, walking among them? Or the son of a god? She'd never thought such beauty could exist, even when she'd danced in the ecstasies of the Goddess under the trees of the sacred grove. He stood head and shoulders over his companions; he glowed with health and strength. Ariadne's father and mother, her sisters, the other Athenians, the court officials and the slaves, all looked insignificant beside him. How could the death lottery have fallen on this man, who must be beloved of the gods?

Oh, gods. The tribute. A wave of painful cold ran through her body, like an evil daimon passing over her. This beautiful man was part of the tribute. Tomorrow, Minos' soldiers would take him to the stairs down into the labyrinth, unarmed and helpless. She and the Minotaur would be waiting at the altar in the centre of the maze, armed and ready to perform the yearly sacrifice.

She couldn't kill this man. She *wanted* him more than she'd ever wanted anyone, or anything. She had to have him.

She knew what she needed to do. She would save him from the sacrifice. He would marry her, and take her away from her father's court. Of course he would want her; men had always wanted her. She had to talk to him.

The speeches were finally over; soon they would all feast together—though the thought of food made Ariadne ill. She was dizzy with desire as the whole party, Minos' court and Athenians alike, moved in an interminable procession from the Great Room to the stone altar outside the palace.

There, Ariadne stood watching her father and mother sacrifice the cattle for the feast in honour of the tribute. The gilded horns of two spotless white heifers and a huge, glossy black bull, the best of

Minos' herd, shone in the harsh noon sun as garlanded women led them into the courtyard. Minos used a double-axe to stun each beast with a blow between the shoulder blades before Pasiphae slit its throat over the altar of mighty Zeus and his earth-shaking brother Poseidon. With each death, sticky rivulets of blood ran down the dark stone.

The sun flashed from Pasiphae's sharp bronze knife into Ariadne's eyes, and her family and the nobles gossiped all around her, but she all she could see or think about was the god-like Athenian, over on the far side of the courtyard. *She had to have him.*

"What are you looking at?" her sister Phaedra whispered.

"Nothing." Ariadne's skin was burning.

"It's that Athenian, isn't it? King Aegeus' son, Theseus."

"They're all the same to me," Ariadne lied. "Which one do you mean?"

Phaedra raised her eyebrows. "You can't be serious. The tall one, over to the left, standing like a real prince. The *beautiful* one. He's the son of King Aegeus, apparently—but the slaves say he's really the child of Poseidon."

The son of a god? No wonder he was so beautiful. She wanted him even more, if that were possible. "If he's Aegeus' son, what's he doing as part of the tribute?" Ariadne said, trying hard to keep her voice level. "Surely the king of Athens could have kept him out of the lottery."

"King Aegeus couldn't stop him, they say. He's brave. He wants to be a hero. He wants to kill the Minotaur and stop the tribute forever."

Ariadne could keep this beautiful man safe from tomorrow's sacrifice, even ask Theodora to spirit them both away. But if he was determined to attack her huge half-brother, he was doomed. "He . . ."

Phaedra nodded. "I know. He hasn't got a chance against our half-brother."

Ariadne's heart pounded.

"You look as if you're going to faint, or something," Phaedra said.

"I'm going over to speak to the Athenians," she said, carefully. Surely it was her right to speak to anyone she wished, even those who were soon to die. In fact, it was probably her duty as a princess.

"I know who you want to talk to." Phaedra winked. "He's been looking at you."

Theseus grinned in the gloom of the labyrinth. It wasn't as dark down here as he'd expected; moonlight shone down through cunning windows in the ceiling, and oil lamps burned on the walls. He'd never dared to hope that it would be so easy. He was going to be a real hero: kill the monster and stop this barbarous tribute forever. And all with the help of Minos' own lovely daughter!

"Just wait here, Theseus, my love," the princess said. "Don't make a sound. You don't want to make him angry." She pressed her thumbnail into the wax of two candles, lit them both, and gave him one. "When the candle has burnt down this far, follow the thread into the maze, and you will find the monster."

"You said you would give me a weapon," he said.

The girl was tying one end of a ball of dark thread to the bars of the gate she'd unlocked for them. She smiled up at him—the princess really was very pretty—and lifted her flounced skirt high. Just as he was about to protest that there'd be time for that sort of thing later, he saw the flash of bronze—a sword in a fine scabbard.

When he held it in his hands, he felt complete once more. "And you're sure the monster is unarmed?" he asked, though at that moment he felt as if he could defeat an army single-handed.

"He has no weapons. And don't worry, I will distract him. You will be able to creep up on us and ambush him."

"Wonderful girl," he said. "A god must have guided me to find you."

"You *will* marry me when we get to Athens, won't you, Theseus?"

Was that a trace of a pout he saw around her lovely mouth? "Of course I will," Theseus said. "How could I resist such a beautiful princess?"

He couldn't really marry her, though, no matter what he'd said to her. Her father King Minos would not make a good ally, if Theseus succeeded in the task he'd set himself, and the girl would bring no rich dowry to the Athenian throne.

No matter. Theseus had already sworn to marry her, and would swear again and again, if that was what it took to buy her help. Anything could happen on the way back to Athens.

Ariadne walked into the labyrinth, her head held high, leaving a trail of thread behind her. Theseus watched her, amazed at his good luck. Perhaps his mother had told the truth; perhaps Poseidon Earth-shaker really *was* his father.

The Minotaur waited in his twilight prison for his last moments with his loveliest, his favourite sister. If bulls could weep, he would have wept.

He heard Ariadne's soft footsteps approaching him, effortlessly finding the fastest path to him. She'd always been able to seek him out, sense him through walls and winding turns. Old Theodora was right; they were linked by the Goddess. He'd always known, though, that she meant much more to him than he did to her.

He knew exactly what she wanted. He was nothing to her, now; less than nothing. He had felt, more than heard, her as she gave the sword to the hero who'd come here to free the Athenians from the tribute. What could that possibly mean for him but death?

Soon, her lovely face appeared around the corner. "There you are, brother," she said, and ran to his arms. Was it only so he could not see betrayal on her face?

He put his huge, horned head down into her hair and breathed in her summery scent. He must cherish each of these last moments.

Too soon, she stepped out of his arms. "Let's go to the old altar," she said with a bright smile, and took his hand. In the other hand, she held the end of a ball of thread and a small candle.

He didn't ask why, or look into her eyes. He'd heard what she'd said to Theseus. What point was there in living, now? He held her soft little hand in his huge one as they walked the winding path to the stone altar of the Goddess.

She put the candle and the thread down on the ground and sat next to them, with her back against the black stone. "Come, Asterion, put your head into my lap," she said. "Just like old times."

The Minotaur could hear the Athenian breathing, where Ariadne had left him at the stairs. There was no need to look at the candle, to see how far it had burned. He would know when the hero started to move.

Ariadne was stroking the fur on his huge, horned head. Did she know that he knew? Was she ashamed?

He would not make it harder for her.

Theseus rounded the final corner, and saw Ariadne sitting with her back to an old stone altar. The unnatural bull-headed monster's head was in her lap, and she was stroking its disgustingly hairy ears, slowly and quietly. How brave she was, doing this for him.

She looked up at Theseus. Her beautiful face was glowing with happiness. "Here is the Minotaur for you, my love," she said. Then she spoke to the monster, its head still in her lap: "You won't resist, will you, Asterion? You want me to be happy, don't you?"

The ghastly monster stood, without a sound. Its human body had looked small, compared with the hideous bull's head set on it, but it was huge. Surely it was a head taller than the tallest man Theseus had ever met—and with such shoulders, such a chest. Those horns were as long and as sharp as bronze daggers. It could spit him in seconds.

Theseus' blood froze in his veins. This would be no easy victory, even if the monster had no metal weapons—but Theseus was a hero. He must stand and fight. He took a step forwards, gripping the sword tightly.

The half-bull turned and stood with its back to Theseus, its sickeningly hairy head stretched out over the stone altar. Was this some kind of trick? The monster would not succeed! So many young Athenians had been sacrificed to this horrendous monster.

Watching the Minotaur for the slightest sign of motion, Theseus strode the few paces to the altar, and swung the sword high in the air.

The beast did not move.

Theseus swung again and again into the human flesh below the monstrous head, severing the thick bones of the spine. Rivers of blood ran down the black stone of the altar. He felt a little ill, but he kept hacking until it was done. Finally, the neck was completely severed. The Minotaur was dead at last. No more young Athenians would die. He had triumphed.

The princess sighed. "Poor Asterion; he always did anything I asked him to. But it's probably better this way. He would never have been happy without me."

What was the girl carrying on about? No matter. Theseus wanted to scream with joy. He'd killed the Minotaur! He was a hero!

"Just leave the body here," the princess said. "Theodora will find it in the morning, when she brings his breakfast. She will arrange the funeral, and all the rituals."

Why couldn't the girl just rejoice at his success? He was a monster-killer. Wandering poets would sing epic songs about him, grandfathers would tell tales of his prowess around the fire, his rivals would envy him, his father would finally look at him with admiration.

The girl said, "And, now, we'd better get your friends free, and escape from the palace. You *will* marry me, when we get back to Athens, won't you?"

Theseus just smiled.

Ariadne stood on the island's narrow beach, watching the Athenian ship disappearing in the distance. They had put into the island of Dia for fresh water, after their escape from burning Knossos. Ariadne had fallen asleep on the warm sand, her head in Theseus' lap, and woken alone, to see the ship receding from her.

"Theseus!" she called again, as she'd called so many times since she woke. But all she heard was the sound of the waves, and the cries of the animals in the trees behind her. Soon the sun would set, and she would be alone here in the dark.

Surely there was some mistake. Surely Theseus could not be so heartless as to leave her here alone, after all she'd done for him.

About the Author:

Jenny is an award-winning Australian writer and poet. Her poems and stories have appeared in Asimov's Science Fiction, Cosmos, Westerly, Strange Horizons *and many more Australian and international journals and anthologies. Legendary feminist writer Pamela Sargent called her novella set in ancient Greece,* The Priestess and the Slave, *"elegant".* *She won two prizes in the Sisters in Crime Australia Scarlet Stiletto awards 2016 for a murder mystery set in classical Delphi, with water nymphs. Eagle Books published her spidery, ghostly middle-grade novel* The Girl in the Mirror *in October 2019. Pitt Street Poetry published* The Duties of a Cat *in 2013,* The Loyalty of Chickens *in 2017, and her third poetry collection,* The Alpaca Cantos, *in April 2020.*

Website www.jennyblackford.com
Twitter @dutiesofacat
Facebook https://www.facebook.com/jennyblackford

DISPLEASURE OF THE GODS

P.A. Mason

Alu stared at the horns, at once too frightened to anoint them for fear of invoking the gods' wrath.

"Quick girl." Fergal poked her in the ribs. "The artefacts wait on no virgin."

Alu gritted her teeth and dipped her fingers into the blood. It was yet warm, and she traced lines from the skull to the horn's tip.

"Don't be stingy girl. More."

Alu cringed under his stare, mortified at the scrutiny. She worked faster, smearing the blood until each horn glistened.

"Enough. Go now." Fergal shoved her shoulder, and she scampered out of the tent, making for the small stream across the field.

She tried not to look at them. They sat around the master harpist, Cormac, and lounged in the sun being instructed on their duties to the divine. The virgin brides, girls from the town selected for their purity and fertility.

A wave of giggles reached her ears, and she hastened to the trees. Her part in the rites was explained to them. As a girl child born of the rites, it was her duty to offer blood of the womb to the divine mask of the bull.

Alu dropped to her knees by the water and scrubbed her hands, wrinkling her nose. It was her first year taking part in the rites, and when she learned what they expected of her, it had terrified her.

"It is your duty to the gods, child." Kellis had said. "We ask for fertility in the fields and in the bellies of our livestock, the gods will not heed our calls if we don't sate their bloodlust."

Aside from the poor beast that represented the gods in the rites, it was only Alu's blood being offered in exchange for their favour. If it satisfied, birthing blood will flow come autumn.

I should count my blessing that birthing is not my part to play, Alu thought.

She dried her hands on her apron and sent a small prayer to the gods into the wind. Raised amongst priestesses, many of her companions had been used to such ends in other rites less revered amongst the townsfolk.

Alu had found no friends amongst the girls now cloistered in the settlement to prepare for their initiation to the divine. Although born of the rites, her gender afforded no status. She was given as a babe to the priestesses where she toiled and received little education in their mysticism. She was another pair of hands, and after this she would return to her drudgery.

Her sleeping quarters neared those of the girls, and she had overheard them whispering at night, excited about their prospects in marriage should they produce a male child.

Good luck to them. Alu thought. *May they enjoy their future in endless childbed.*

Snatching a basket from behind a hut, Alu set off across the field toward the boggy marshes to gather reeds for the workhouse. She glanced toward Cormac who looked irritated at her disruption of his herd of virgins.

What measures would the druids take to ensure a good omen following years of near famine? She wondered.

It was no secret that the druids rutted with them relentlessly following the rites, to spur on the seed of the divine, or so they said. If babes were born of the union, the townsfolk would rejoice and look ahead to a bountiful year and cease their dark muttering about the druids. They considered this year particularly fortuitous, the male child of such a union was now at his majority, set to take his place in the hall of the gods.

"Alu."

She hefted the basket overhead, determined not to slow down.

"Alu, wait." Fintan's voice rang out behind her.

"Not now, Fintan. I have work yet to do."

She'd been avoiding him for weeks. Since his role in the rites was made clear, he had been preening like a peacock and making her life miserable. The young boy who'd been her playmate was now gone, instead a young man, tall and intimidating, stalked her around their settlement. She set off down the slope without a backwards glance until she felt the basket ripped from her arms.

"Let me carry that for you." Fintan tucked the basket under an arm and flashed a dazzling smile. "You have anointed them, then?"

She felt her cheeks burn, was her part known to everyone?

"The artefacts have been prepared." She kept her tone aloof, as if that could save her dignity.

Fintan grinned. "Then you have no excuses left. You cannot tell me you don't envy them." He nodded toward the girls, their eyes now following Fintan.

"I would hate to see your divine seed go to waste; they seem a greedy bunch." She yanked the basket from Fintan and trotted off down the hillside, ignoring the giggles from behind her.

Alu breathed a sigh of relief when she reached the marshes and the blessed quiet surrounding them. She tied her skirts up around her knees and pulled a small knife from her belt to cut reeds down at the muddy stems. It was a chore she enjoyed, away from scolding priestesses, and whilst dirty, was less foetid than other tasks given when in disfavour.

The rites were less than a week away, and in that time her womb would cease bleeding. Alu resolved to avoid Fintan where she could, she may be unable to keep him off her now she had served her celestial purpose.

He had been strutting around like a randy goat for months, gloating over his own misguided sense of virility, looking at girls like prey. Although off limits, he made no secret of coveting Alu's virginity which he declared would doubly ensure the gods favour.

Alu grunted as she cut through swathes of reeds, her frustration bent to her task. It was preposterous. She lived amongst a group of superstitious fools who knew no more of the gods will than the tadpoles swimming around her feet. She had known lean years when the rites had promised a bounty and full bellies but instead brought crippling blight. Other years where food was plentiful and the omens were ill favoured. Alu didn't understand why the townsfolk endured it.

Except perhaps the wine, she conceded.

Home to the oldest vines with the sweetest grapes, their fields exported rich barrels that saw the town prosper even when there was little in places nearby. Especially coveted was the rare vintage mixed with sacred essence which gave even a king the finest of dreams.

But the vineyard remained sparse and had for almost four years. Nobody knew why, the vines were in good health, greenery spread each year, but the fruit sprang only in small bunches.

With her basket now full, Alu trudged back up to the huts, balancing the basket over her shoulder. Light waned, and smoke began to billow out from the stone stacked chimneys. Winter's bite was receding, but the night air yet brought frost along with it.

"Think of the wine, Alu. The winter was bitter, new barrels will put everyone in good cheer." Niamh pulled weeds alongside Alu with vigour.

"I saw Seafraid and Fergal arguing when he brought up the wagon yesterday. He says the rites are too lavish." Alu tore at a weed and caught her finger on a prickle.

"Seafraid would have the wealth of the town to himself, he was always mean spirited." Niamh chuckled. "And it is his daughter that is chosen this year. I heard they keep a strange priest in their house."

Alu had seen the priest. He had a sour face and had scowled at her when she had brought a small cask to Seafraid's home. He had uttered a word, *blaspheme,* but when she asked Kellis later about its meaning, she only clouted her and told her to get back to work.

"Sadb seems happy enough to perform her duties." Niamh scoffed. "Those girls have done nothing but sat on their arses making eyes at Cormac for a full week now. Likely when everybody is doing the work around here, he is giving them explicit instruction to prepare them." Niamh made a face and a crude gesture before standing up, waving at her to stay kneeling. "The weeds won't pull themselves out, Alu. I've to check on the dyes." Niamh trudged off leaving Alu staring at her hands.

With a grunt she wiped her hand on her apron and returned to the task, endless at this time of year with unwanted greenery crowding the vegetable gardens. She couldn't explain the sense of unease at the impending rites, or the subtle signs of unrest between the townsfolk and the druids. Fergal muttered about the lack of respect afforded to him, but Alu couldn't remember a time that was any different. She was now in her fourteenth year and Fergal had little colour left in his scrappy beard.

With the gardens cleared, she made off for the middens where other refuse will next year provide nourishment to the fields. The great silver circle, the turning of life from one year to the next, ever rolling forward. Alu received no instruction from the priestesses, but they never knew when she lingered outside their tents at night listening to stories of the gods and the marks they left on the world. Part of Alu wanted to believe that it was Arianrhod who would answer to the rites, but she feared it was all tales of fairies, told to keep children obedient and townsfolk from despair.

She wrinkled her nose as she approached the middens, far from the village huts. Alu could see the line of trees that marked the edge of the Groves and thought she saw a deer skip by. Her eyes flickered across the wall of trees and she jumped at a set of eyes staring at her.

One of the townsfolk's cattle, what was the stupid beast doing in the Groves? Alu frowned, the stare seemed so unlike the vacant eyes of the stout shaggy creatures kept by the townsfolk. Her heartbeat sounded in her ears and she tore her gaze away to run back to the huts. As she neared the settlement Fintan stepped into her path.

"What has you running in here like a banshee?" He wore the stupid grin that had scarce left his face all week. "Has your womb dried up enough to take your pleasure?"

"Not now, Fintan. One of the beasts has escaped, it's up in the Grove." She made to push past him.

"What were you doing in the Groves?" He took a sidestep and held an arm up to bar her path.

"I was at the middens, the stupid creature was staring at me from the trees." Alu ducked under his arm and ran toward the huts, dropping her basket along the way.

When she burst into the priestesses' workhouse, heads snapped toward her.

"What is it, child?" Kellis frowned over her weaving.

"The Groves. One of the town folks' cattle." Her breath came short, and she held a hand to her chest. "It must have wandered off."

Kellis nodded to the boy stacking wood into the hearth. "Go tell Seafraid, boy."

The boy turned, it was Timeas, and scuttled out past her.

"You were in the Groves?" Kellis' voice was sharp.

"No. I was at the middens, it was staring at me from the trees. It was strange." Alu caught herself and turned her eyes to the floor. "Forgiveness Kellis. I should not interrupt your work."

"We need more reeds, child. Go."

When she looked up, Kellis was giving her a peculiar stare.

Alu knew better than to tarry, and trotted back out through the huts, collecting her basket along the way. She saw Timeas across the field, running like the wind. Losing a beast that had survived the winter would be a bad omen, but Fergal would bristle at having men with their dogs tramping through the Groves so near to the rites.

I hope I saw it in truth. Alu swallowed.

It wouldn't be the first fanciful tale she had told the priestesses, more often than not it ended with a clout over the ear and weeks doing the worst of the chores.

Her feet carried her swiftly to the marshes, doubt winding its way into her mind. She could not shift the growing worry nestled deep in her belly, despite the growing cheer of those around her. She wanted no more than to hide, to be spirited far from this place.

"Tell us again girl." Fergal waved the smoking bundle of herbs under her nose and tightened his grip in Alu's hair. She took a ragged gasp against the white smoke filling her nose.

"I didn't see much, it was in the woods, a bull, it was staring at me." Alu coughed and spluttered.

"There were no beasts missing, stupid girl. Tell us what you saw." Fergal had been interrogating her for what seemed like hours. He was in a foul mood; men had been scouring the Groves in the hope there was a beast from another settlement which wandered off.

"It was white, I think. Big horns." Alu cringed when Fergal twisted his hand, winding her hair tighter.

"White? There are no white cattle this side of the river." He thrust her away. "You were ever more trouble than you were worth."

"Arianrhod." Kellis sat close to the hearth and swung her gaze to Fergal.

"You think the goddess would choose this wretch to show herself to?" Fergal spat.

"Of course not. But the townsfolk will if we tell them so." Kellis narrowed her eyes at Alu. "Give her the wine, she will spout the same babble. Seafraid won't be able to convince the others if we tell them this year will be especially blessed."

"We mock the gods to earn the favour of those who would turn their back on them. As if it weren't the gods themselves who gave us the secrets of the wine." Fergal began pacing the small hut. Alu sat cringing, forgotten for now.

"We must do what is necessary to survive. They would forget the gods without us." Kellis stared into the fire.

"Christians. The omens became darker when those priests washed up on our shores. They would have folk fasting when they should be feasting, repenting when they should be revelling. What do they know of the stars? Of what is owed when the bull is above us?" He stopped to inhale the bundle of herbs.

"We have a male child born of the rites this year, Fintan will play his part as the horned one well. And we now have a daughter of the rites who has seen a mystical bull." Kellis turned her gaze to Alu with mockery in her eyes. "Folks will remember the old ways. None will keep themselves closeted for long when there is wine and fertility to honour."

Fergal spun to face Alu, looking down at her with a scowl. "Did you hear that, girl? A magnificent white bull. Arianrhod come to bless us all with ripe fields and fat livestock. If you say any different, I will nourish the fields with your blood."

Alu squeaked and nodded, the close confines and the hazy smoke made her head spin.

"Go, child." Kellis waved toward the door and Alu scrambled.

Her feet carried her through the darkness toward the middens, far away from the others. It was yet dark, but the moon was full enough to light the way ahead. She sat slumped on an accommodating log with her face buried in her hands.

Stupid beast. Fergal's ire was notorious, she knew she would be in disfavour for a long time yet. She had never drunk the nectar of the gods, what if she said the wrong thing? She had watched the rites from afar in years gone by, people stumbled around uninhibited, either raving or rutting. The thought of what Fintan would do should he find her in that state curdled her stomach. Fergal would do nothing to stop it.

Something caught Alu's eye, and she looked up into the treeline. A strange light glowed from the Groves. It was blue and bright, no orange flicker from a torch. The townsfolk would be safely tucked in their beds by now, the settlement behind her seemed restful. Alu unfolded herself and backed away. When the light extinguished, she turned and fled back to her cot.

The morning was met with the bustle of preparation for the rites. Effigies were carried out and strung from stakes and woven garlands adorned them as they stood sentinel over the slope. Barrels were brought up and blessed by the priests and a growing excitement wounds its way amongst the settlement's inhabitants. They would hold the rites tomorrow under the stars. Alu fled to the marshes where she hoped they would forget her.

With the effigies in place, the need for reeds diminished and Alu collected roots and plants that would make medicines for the townsfolk they traded with beyond the grassy plains. She should be in the gardens at this time of year, but it was too near the huts for comfort. She had left her bed in near darkness before anyone could give her instructions.

The birds of the marsh seemed no less excited, they accepted her presence amongst them and seemed playful that morning, chasing each other around and squawking. Alu smiled despite herself, she often wished she could enjoy the freedom of the wild creatures she worked alongside.

"Alu." She turned to see young Timeas run down the slope toward her. "Fergal is looking for you, you must go with him to Flintwood. He goes to meet with the council."

Alu's blood ran cold. So there was no hiding then.

"You best go, he is in a foul temper." Timeas nodded toward her basket. "I will bring that back."

Alu nodded to Timeas and held her skirts up as she dashed toward the huts. She found Fergal standing beside the wagon, barrels of the new vintage stacked high.

"And where have you been, girl?" His face was mottled and red. "You think the high priest of this place waits on the likes of you?"

Alu lowered her gaze. "Forgiveness."

He thrust a cup under her chin and Alu took a step backward.

"Drink girl, mystical dreams await." Fergal glared at her and she bit her lip, holding a shaking hand out.

The wine was sickly sweet with an undernote of something earthy. Despite growing up in the settlement, Alu knew nothing of what went into the wine brewed by the priests. Fergal tilted the cup upward and Alu choked down the wine, terrified of spilling the godly vintage.

"Now hop in the back of the wagon. Mind yourself, or I will tie you down." Fergal turned to bark orders at the boys milling around and Alu climbed in amongst the stacked barrels.

With more shouts, the lads whipped the oxen into a grunting amble and the wagon creaked into movement. Alu turned her gaze up to the sky and rested her head back against an accommodating sack. The trip to Flintwood would take some hours yet, her wits were likely to be addled by the time she saw the small houses.

Her mind already had begun to cloud, she felt as though strange threads were being wound around her, her eyes twisting the clouds above her head. The sounds of Fergal and the lads dwindled, as though they were far away and not stumbling alongside the wagon. Fear melted and gave way to a daze that brought a smug grin to her face, the gods must favour her if the wine brought contentment.

Whispers. Like the nattering of birds, but in a language she had never heard before. When she felt close enough to grasp what they were saying they slipped again, a foreign tongue which sounded lyrical, even to her uninitiated ears.

Do the gods chatter in my ear? What would they have me do? Alu blinked, trying to regain focus, but slipped back into a thoughtless dream.

When the oxen halted, Alu's eyes snapped open, broken from the reverie she had become lost in. She had not noticed the sounds of a bustling town around her, nor the smells that lingered where people gathered. Fergal began shouting orders to the lads and by the time he stuck his head over the back of the wagon Alu had sat up, her head swimming.

"Get up, girl. Time for you to meet with the council."

Alu shuffled off the end of the wagon and held to the straps to keep her feet from falling under her. Some townsfolk helped unload and others milled around chattering about the strange folk that lived in the hills. Fergal grasped Alu by the arm and hauled her along to the building up ahead, one of the few made with stone.

"Now mind what you say, the council were displeased they wasted a good day stomping around looking for a mythical bull." Fergal grip tightened. "You will do as instructed."

The silly beast, why did it wander off? The lights. Arianrhod, the gods.

Alu mumbled assent.

Fergal thrust her ahead of him through the door and Alu's vision swam as she cast her eyes across the men seated around the hearth. He pushed Alu to her knees beside the doorway.

"Fergal." Seafraid's voice dripped with scorn. "Come to beg forgiveness after yesterday's hunt?"

Alu noticed the priest sitting in the corner, glaring at her and making signs of the cross.

"I must apologise yes, but only for mistaking the omens. The gods speak to this one." Fergal nodded toward Alu. "We found her dancing under the light of the moon, communing with Arianrhod herself."

Seafraid barked a laugh. "More nonsense. Tell us, what did this goddess have to say to that whelp?"

The other men chuckled. Fergal cleared his throat.

"It was indeed a bull the girl saw. Might I remind you this one was born of the rites, it is her blood that nourishes the bull's mantle. Arianrhod has decreed a bountiful year should homage be paid to her in the womb of this one."

The words washed over Alu, she stared into the fire which seemed to spill from the hearth and dance along the walls.

"I'm sure there is no shortage of pricks on the hill to fill her belly," Seafraid sneered. "What of the day our men spent away from their work?"

"The bull was sent as an omen. It is not a priest that Arianrhod seeks, but a hunter. She requires a virile man, one proven to be a master of the woods." Fergal waved his arms at the skins adorning the floors and walls. "She calls you, Seafraid, to honour her."

Seafraid rubbed his chin, at once sober and the other men crowded around began muttering.

"Blaspheme." The priest in the corner stood and pointed to Fergal. "You would have the good folk of this town pay homage to wicked creatures under the moonlight. Fornicating out of blessed wedlock, honouring the devil himself."

Alu blinked. *What is it Fergal wants of Seafraid?*

The cloak billowed around the priest, Alu saw smoke rising from the sombre outfit, dancing in lazy circles around him.

"These people have honoured the gods long before your kind made it to these shores, priest." Fergal spat. "Would the folk here deny the gods and welcome a year of poverty?"

"The vineyard looks to be scant again this year, Fergal." Another man stood and stoked the fire. "You would have us believe the rites will bring good fortune after such a decline?"

"The gods test us. His presence." Fergal pointed at the priest. "Angers them. He would deny their very existence."

Seafraid lurched from his chair and strode to Alu, his hand reaching into her hair to lift her face toward him.

"And what say you, girl? What drivel would you spout after drinking the wine?"

Stupid beast. The Groves. Lights. Leave me alone.

"Arianrhod." Alu muttered. "The beast, lights. In the Groves."

"This one is senseless." Seafraid thrust Alu to the floor and turned to the men. "Are we to turn our backs on the true god on the word of a druid and a girl in the throes of a wicked brew?"

Muttering filled the room, and another man stood, pushing his chair out from behind him. "The folk of this town care not for your god, Seafraid. The rites are older than the town itself. If you are not man enough to take your place, I will honour Arianrhod."

Alu started at the eruption of shouting in the room, her mind swam as the men argued and she held a hand to her belly.

"The town trusts in my leadership, Ricard. Dare you challenge me?" Seafraid blocked Alu's view.

"Turn your back on the old ways and the folk here will rise against you. They will string your precious priest up amongst the effigies." Ricard pushed past Seafraid and knelt down by Alu, holding her chin.

"Tell us what you saw, girl." He tucked Alu's hair behind her ear.

"A white bull, Arianrhod. Lights. In the Groves." Alu stared into Ricard's eyes, they swam in fire and light.

"Ignore the gods at your own peril, Seafraid. This girl sees visions, I will honour Arianrhod if you dare scorn her."

Alu sank down when Ricard let go of her chin and the room melted away from her view. *The beast. The lights. In the Groves. Arianrhod.*

Alu woke in a different hut, her head pounding. Glancing around, she saw the cots of the other girls brought to the hill to prepare for their sacrifice. Her belly sour, her mouth dry, Alu lurched up and pushed out of the doorway to seek water.

The morning was young, fog shrouded the hills and there was calm in the settlement, at least for now. Alu trotted over to the stream and dropped her face down to drink. Her thirst slaked, she wiped her mouth and lay on the lush grass hugging the embankment.

The town, the council. Memory swirled in her mind, as elusive as smoke. Her part was done, then. Alu wiped her eyes and stretched her limbs. Morning. The rites were tonight.

Alu sat up, alarmed, and pushed herself up to trot back to the settlement. The priests would be closeting themselves in preparation, the priestesses anointing the girls and giving their blessings. That left Alu to go about her work in peace. She made her way by the privies before gathering her basket, if she got down to the marshes she may be forgotten entirely.

"Alu." She turned to see Kellis standing at the threshold to the priestesses' workhouse. "Come."

Alu cursed and turned back, dropping her basket by the door before following Kellis inside. The girls lounged around on woven mats attended by priestesses adorning their bodies with ritual markings. Kellis looked at her expectantly.

"Forgiveness. I slept late, what do you wish of me?" Alu turned her eyes downward and the girls erupted into giggles.

"You must prepare for the rites, child. We must at least have you look the part." Kellis brushed a hand over Alu's hair. "Although I am not sure there are enough hours this day to get those tangles from your hair."

Alu's head snapped up, confused. "Prepare?"

Kellis narrowed her eyes and grabbed Alu's chin. "Your eyes are clear, the wine has worn off. What do you remember?"

Alu swallowed, casting her mind back to the council. "I told them. About Arianrhod, the Groves and the bull."

"You played your part, child. But you have work yet to do. We must all make sacrifices." Kellis wrapped an arm around Alu and led her to a trough of water. "Yours will be your virginity."

Kellis unwound the ties that held Alu's smock in place and tugged her garments off. Alu's shivers weren't from the cold. Seafraid. The shouting.

"Get in, child. When was the last time you washed?" Kellis wrinkled her nose and Alu flushed crimson, the girls behind her snorted with laughter.

Alu climbed into the trough, the water now cool, and dropped into the water, burying her head in her hands. *What have I done?* Alu's frame began to heave silent sobs.

Hands thrust into the surrounding water, coarse linen scrubbed at her body and hair.

When Alu looked up, she saw other priestesses crowding around the trough, no hint of sympathy in their eyes. She allowed herself to be prodded and scoured, a sense of defeat growing in her belly.

They didn't believe me, why would they mock the gods and include me in the rites?

"Now girls, you must be willing in your sacrifice." Kellis droned. "The bull will not care, willing or not, but Arianrhod will bless those who are eager in the rites with a full womb."

The priestesses drew back and held up a wrap, nodding at Alu to get out of the water.

She swallowed and wiped her face before climbing out, shivering as the wrap enshrouded her.

"There are six of you, and each of you will need to encourage him to share his seed." Kellis strode around to check on the markings winding their way across their bellies. "You have until dawn before the rites conclude."

The priestesses rubbed Alu vigorously and brought over a blue wrap to wind around her breasts and rump. She was pushed down onto the mats and combs snared at her hair.

Kellis turned her gaze toward her. "You are uninitiated, it can't be helped. Your sacrifice to Seafraid will be witnessed by the townspeople, and with it, they will once again show proper respect for the gods." She bent to narrow her eyes at her. "You will go eagerly to the rites, it may yet earn favour with Fergal. If I were you, I would not risk his displeasure a second time."

Alu shuddered and nodded, turning her gaze down while the priestesses pulled at her hair. She had seen only seen a sacrifice given publicly once. The druids preferred secrecy and mysticism when it came to the rites, only showing enough to the townsfolk to satisfy superstition. As soon as their dance was done, Fintan would gather his virgins and take them to the groves. The rest would be left to the druid's mutterings and blessings.

"I must attend to the artefacts, you girls will turn your thoughts to prayer." Kellis swept out of the workhouse, and tears spilled from Alu's eyes.

"My father will be angry indeed, having to rut with that creature." Sadb glared at Alu. "He almost refused Fergal when I was called."

"He cannot call you back now, Sadb." Eimear stroked her back. "When you bear a male child, he will be happy enough. You will make a good match for Cillian."

Alu hunched over, wishing herself invisible. The rites were as much a sport for the virgins as the bull. If Alu produced a child, it would afford no prospects, she would lie down in childbed and if she was fortunate enough to survive would be put back to work.

Alu stopped listening to the girls' chatter and retreated into her own thoughts as the priestesses brought out blue dye to paint her belly, arms and face with the ritual markings.

Here I was worried about what Fintan was likely to do to me.

Alu recalled rough hands in her hair, being thrust to the floor.

Being compelled to take part in the rites, Seafraid would be none too gentle.

A sharp sting smarted her thigh.

"Enough tears, girl. You will ruin the dye." Mabh glared down at her, she was ever in a foul temper, one of the older priestesses in the settlement.

Alu sniffled and carefully drew fingers across her eyes.

"You are a daughter of the rites; your virginity belongs to the gods. Did you not think to when you would be called to make that sacrifice?" Mabh tittered. "If you please the gods, they may make a priestess of you yet."

Mabh began drawing lines across Alu's face and muttering under her breath.

A priestess? Me? Not likely.

"They will give you the wine, child," Mabh whispered. "If you are fortunate, you won't even recall it come dawn."

Alu tried to keep her face still whilst the priestess worked, studying the deep lines on her face. Mabh was not one to show the younger ones kindness. Alu couldn't remember a time when the woman had looked young.

"Girl children of the fertility rites are not shown proper respect in this place." Mabh ran a line up her cheek and gave a small nod to herself. "You saw the bull, girl. I doubt it not that Arianrhod has plans for you."

Alu swallowed, unable to respond.

Mabh drew away, leaving Alu alone amid bustling priestesses and mindless chatter.

Alu traced the blue lines which spread across her belly with her fingertip. Fasting did not aid her sour belly, she felt more nauseous than she had that morning. The others ignored her for the most part, which suited her. She sat away from the hearth, not bothered by the drought coming from the doorway.

From outside the workhouse, the sounds of arriving townsfolk making ready grew steadily. There would be feasting that night and they brought offerings in gratitude for the wine delivered to them. The special vintage would flow even before the rites began, adding mysticism to the rituals that followed.

A drum sounded and Alu startled. The druids of the hill honoured music and would fill the night air with rhythmic drumming, for now there was a general cacophony of instruments being tested and carried out to the hillside.

On edge, Alu muttered about needing the privies and ducked out of the workhouse, slinking against the buildings to creep away from those going about their preparations. She had not bothered with her smock for fear of smudging the dye, and the crisp air against her bare skin sent shivers down her limbs.

Alu let out a small sigh as she rounded the back of the settlement, now alone with her own thoughts, when her arm was grabbed from behind.

"Clever plan, Alu." Fintan swung her around, his fingers biting into her arm. "Thought you would deny me? Devise some silly vision and demand a place in the rites?"

Alu froze, eyes darting.

"If the gods truly wanted a blessed union it would be of two children of the rites." Fintan leered at her, Alu smelt wine on his breath.

"You wouldn't." Alu's lip trembled.

"Seafraid isn't like to know one way or the other." Fintan grabbed at the blue wrap, tearing.

Alu let out a scream before Fintan pushed his mouth against hers, muffling her outburst. He pushed her backward in his embrace and she stumbled back over the grassy hill toward the treeline. His grip tightened on her arm and she clamped her eyes shut, now swimming with tears.

"Fintan." It was Niamh's voice, although Alu couldn't see her.

Fintan tore his lips from hers and turned toward the huts. "Be off, woman. Who are you to disrupt my pleasure? I represent the gods this day."

"Mark me, I will call it from the hillside if you deflower that girl. Gods or no, Fergal will have your prick for it," Niamh hissed. "Save your seed for the rites. If you are fortunate Fergal may let you have her after your work is done."

Alu trembled and Fintan thrust her away before turning to storm off. Alu sank to her knees, racked with silent sobs.

"There, now." Niamh crouched beside her. "Look what you've done, the markings will need to be fixed." Niamh dabbed at Alu's face with her apron to halt the damage.

"He wouldn't, would he? Fergal?" Alu's eyes searched Niamh's, yet she already knew the answer.

"You know what the priests' workhouse sounds like for the week after the rites. It's worse than a stag's rutting season. It may be kinder yet for Fintan to wear himself out with you." Niamh's eyes softened. "I know it is frightening, but you sacrifice your virginity only once. If you are especially blessed, there will be no babe to come and you can forget it ever happened."

Niamh helped Alu up and brushed off the dirt and grass stuck to her legs. "Now come with me, I have some dye by the kitchens, we can clean you up there, nobody will need know this happened."

Alu sniffled and nodded, casting her eyes down as she followed Niamh to the kitchens. Niamh was the closest person to a mother Alu had ever known, and even she couldn't protect her from this fate.

Niamh sat Alu down in front of the hearth and handed her a mug of ale. She had no stomach for wine and her belly growled in appreciation.

"I suppose a crust of bread won't hurt." Niamh grinned. "The wine will work well enough." Niamh gathered dye and bread from the table laden with food yet to prepare and Alu extended her feet toward the fire, comforted by the warm glow. Niamh took the mug from Alu's hands and knelt down in front of her to wash away the dirt and trace over the smeared lines.

Alu stuffed the bread in her mouth, she couldn't remember when she last ate.

The dye dried quickly in front of the hearth and Niamh re-wrapped the linen around Alu's frame. She studied her with narrowed eyes and plucked some grass from her hair before giving a sharp nod.

"There. All cleaned up. Now go, the priestesses will be wondering where you got to. Tell them you were with me." Niamh waved her hands and Alu scuttled out the door, this time eager to get to the workhouse where she would be left in peace, at least for now.

On the way back something caught Alu's eye. Her head snapped toward the tree line, there was a blur of white from amongst the trees that disappeared almost as she saw it.

The wine must be lingering in my mind yet.

Alu broke into a trot, mindful of being waylaid a second time.

As the sound outside grew with merriment, Alu began to pace the confines of the workhouse, near panic. The girls had thought nothing of her absence, they hadn't even acknowledged her when she returned. Some of them lay napping and others worked non-existent tangles from their hair.

The smell of roasted meat infiltrated the huts and the odd shout spoke of the townsfolk settling to their cups. Through the doorway, Alu could see the light beginning to wane, it wouldn't be long before the rites would begin.

Expectant or no, Alu startled when the first of the priestesses swept back into the room to check on them. Mabh held a small cask and sat it on a bench to begin pouring.

Kellis was the last to march in, her eyes casting around for any sign of disruption. On her head she wore a mantle, made with reeds and threaded through with the earliest flowers of the season. Although not a tall woman, her presence filled the room.

"It is now time to make the final preparations. You will each be anointed with oils and drink the wine of the gods to better illuminate your presence to them this night." Kellis' eyes found Alu, and she frowned. "You must calm yourself, child."

"You must ask her why she went missing earlier," Sabh drawled. "Much too long for a trip to the privies."

Kellis snapped her head toward Sabh and she shrunk on the mat. Kellis turned her glare to Alu. "Explain."

"Niamh needed help in the kitchens. I wasn't gone long." Alu glanced over the markings entwining her. "I was careful not to ruin the dye."

Kellis glared a moment longer and took a deep breath. "Good. Now, you must each make ready."

The priestesses began fussing over the girls, a basket was pulled over from next to the hearth where similar mantles were handed out and oils brought down from the shelves.

Mabh brought the first cup to Alu and proffered it to her with the barest of smiles. "Drink up, girl," She whispered. "You need a healthier dose than those ones."

Alu's nose wrinkled at the familiar scent, she was thankful for the ale and bread earlier that had calmed her roiling stomach. Taking a deep breath, she took the cup and gulped the wine down. Its effects were hastened this time, the wine that yet flowed in her blood was set alight with the fresh dose.

Mabh attended her, smearing heady oils over her body and pinning the mantle to her hair. She frowned at the small tear in the linen wrapping her body and tucked it away out of sight, saying nothing.

Kellis fetched a bundle of herbs hanging from the rafters and set one end alight in the fire.

Mabh steered Alu to sit amongst the girls on the woven mats and Kellis began encircling them, muttering under her breath. The smoke began to infiltrate the room, lingering in hazy clouds, smothering.

The muttering was picked up by the other priestesses who now surrounded the girls, their incantations rising into a chorus. Alu's head swam, she heard no words, only a seductive melody which drew her mind away from the workhouse, from the girls surrounding her. Her vision slid around the walls, the herbs and jars lining the shelves seemed to jostle.

Alu didn't hear the summons, but when the priestess hauled her up she snapped into focus, the sound of the drums now ringing in her ears. The light filtering through the doorway had dulled. As the priestess drew back the hide covering, Alu saw dusk had settled over the settlement.

The other girls were herded out ahead of Alu and she shifted from foot to foot, trying to keep hold of what little clarity remained. Mabh fussed with her mantle before nudging her out through the doorway with a firm hand on her back.

The smell of the fires and meat reached her first, her stomach growling despite her scant meal earlier. The drums had quieted the hillside, as Alu trailed behind girls she saw townsfolk gathered round the fires and effigies. They looked to Fergal who was arranging artefacts on a table brought out.

Fintan was nowhere to be seen. Alu cast her eyes around and found the creature that he would challenge when the blessings were complete and the effigies lit. Adorned with flowers and dye, the beast nuzzled its handler and received a scratch behind the ear and a crust of bread.

Always the most docile of creatures. Alu smothered a giggle.

Alu halted behind Kellis who took her place by the artefacts. With nothing to grasp, she began to sway in time to the drums, her eyes drawn to the fires which leapt into the air. The wine thrummed through her veins, a sheen of sweat grew on her brow.

When the drums slowed and hushed, Cormac brought his harp forward and dropped his heavy cloak. The firelight illuminated his pale skin, now entangled with intricate markings which wound their way down his arms across his bare chest. He settled onto an ancient stump facing out to the townsfolk and the clear notes of the harp rang out. Whatever sound remained amongst those standing to watch were snuffed out, it was a rare treat to be allowed to listen to the music of the gods.

Cormac's voice rose through the notes with stunning power, wordless, captivating. Priestesses nudged the girls forward, and as each trod off they began to turn and twist in a circle around the fire.

Kellis held a hand out in front of Alu. "Not you, child."

Alu shrank back. Her eye was pulled to the sudden movement amongst the townsfolk. The priest from Seafraid's household. Alu thought she saw a flash of contempt on his face as he turned from the fires and marched off. She hadn't seen Seafraid amongst the crowd.

Perhaps he has refused. Alu blinked, trying to follow her own thoughts.

The Groves loomed far behind the fires and they seemed ominous in the orange glow. Alu remembered the white lights.

It is of little reprieve that I won't be led down that path this night, my offering will be given by the fireside.

Alu's stomach churned and her mouth grew dry.

The harp notes faded, and the girls slowed in their dance, coming to a halt by the effigies strung up at different points of the circle.

"Good folk, I welcome you this night to bear witness to the sacred offerings to the gods." Fergal held his hands up, his voice pitched across the crowd. "With sacrifice comes blessing, in your homes and in the fields. This year brings good fortune, the omens speak of a bountiful year ahead."

Cheers rose from those already ruddy from the wine.

"This year we have both a male and female child of the rites." Fergal flourished a wave toward Alu. "Both will sacrifice themselves on the altar of Arianrhod, representing the great bull in the stars, and in return she will bless us with her favour."

Alu shuddered and shrank from the eyes staring at her. Kellis gave her a sharp poke to the ribs and Alu straightened.

"The great hunter will take part in these rites, Arianrhod's chosen consort. His virility will draw her close, her lust for him will spill into our vineyard and its fruit will hang heavy in the new season."

Fergal nodded to the cluster of priests behind him who snuck away to summon the horned one. He picked up the ritual knife from the artefacts and held it high to cheers. He sliced his palm and clenched his fist before circling the fire, marking each effigy with his blood sacrifice.

Kellis took the knife from Fergal to make her own blood sacrifice. Without so much as a wince, she sliced her hand and approached the bull, now wary with the scent of blood in the air. With long strokes across his horns, she muttered incantations at the creature and stepped aside so it could be led closer to the fires.

There were footfalls behind her and Alu turned to see Fintan approach. With the mantle of the bull in place she scarcely recognised him, his frame seemed larger, the dye traced the veins down his arms. Alu swallowed. Behind him was Seafraid, without the mantle but intimidating, nonetheless.

"The horned one has come and will offer himself as a sacrifice to the gods." Fergal paced in front of the crowd. "Should the gods favour not be with us, they will bid the bull strike him down."

Fintan held his hands up as he approached, and the crowd cheered. The drums sounded again, slow, deliberate. The handler held the beast firm, which had only now become skittish with the sudden cacophony. Fintan brushed past Alu to take his place and Seafraid halted beside her. She glanced at him under lowered lashes and her teeth began to chatter.

Fintan circled the fire before approaching the beast, the drums hastened, he seemed to move in time with them. The milling priests took torches to the fire, and each went to an effigy to set it alight. Fintan called out his challenge.

Alu heard hoofbeats, the sound seemingly coming from within her mind. The beast in the groves. Her mouth agape, she turned to stare toward the treeline, expectant, waiting. She wandered from Seafraid's side to creep closer, her mind filled with the thundering of hooves.

A white light, now bursting from the trees. Too bright to make out the figure in the middle. Alu knew it was the white bull. She tore her gaze to look amongst the crowd. They appeared not to notice, how could they not hear it? She could feel the ground quiver under her feet.

Fintan held his arms up in challenge, his roaring sounding victorious. The beast held by the fireside pulled against its tether, but made no move to strike him down. Surely the creature understood.

A mighty bellow erupted and Alu's head snapped back toward the light, almost upon the ring of effigies. Everything began to slow, Alu licked her lips and backed away from the fires.

The first shouts sounded as the white light breached the circle and the spell in Alu's mind broke. Panic welled up, people began to scatter. From the light emerged the bull, brilliant white, and he lowered his head as he thundered toward Fintan.

Struck dumb, Fintan yet held his arms up.

Move, dullard. Alu's hands reached up to her mouth to smother a scream.

The bull crashed into Fintan, his great horns goring him through the middle. Lifted from the ground, Fintan thrashed and the bull carried him on out of the circle, shaking his head in an attempt to dislodge the screaming man from its horns. As the bull circled round again, a white light erupted from its form, and a woman emerged, striding into the circle. She yanked her arm clear of Fintan's middle, leaving blood and gore smeared over her pristine white gown.

Alu swallowed, frozen in fear. People ran in every direction, screaming.

The woman drew her arms up, holding her head back to cry out. Her scream pierced Alu's very being, she held hands up to her ears with a wince.

Fergal lay flat on the ground, hands over his head.

Alu stared at him, the gods chosen priest, quivering like the lowliest of worms.

The keening stopped, and the woman stalked toward him. "Messenger of the gods. You displease me." Her face filled with contempt as she stared down at him. "I am Arianrhod and you will answer for your crimes this night."

Alu's chest tightened, and she looked around the fires. All the townsfolk had fled, few of the people of the hills remained.

"Mercy, great goddess." Fergal remained on the ground, craning his head to stare at her feet.

"You share the gods secrets with those who would do us harm. The wine of the gods is shared wantonly with those who have coin. You offer as sacrifice that which is not yours to give." Arianrhod snapped her head toward Alu. "Come, child."

Alu started, her eyes growing wide. Her feet moved of their own volition, carrying her toward the deity.

"A child of the rites. My child. Offered to an uninitiated Christian." Arianrhod spat. "And the male child spurred on to take what should be given freely."

Arianrhod turned to stare at Fintan's body. "This one is not mine. He sprang from the seed of priests long after the ritual fires burned out."

"Please, mercy." Fergal had scrambled up, now on his knees with his head bowed. "We have no wish to anger the gods."

Arianrhod ignored him and held out her hand. "Come child. Let us be away from here."

Alu stood frozen save the shaking.

Arianrhod's eyes narrowed, and she dropped her hand. "I will give you a choice. You may yet dwell in the hills with these folk. Your blood would nourish the soil and I will bless the people with a bounty, you would be a great priestess amongst them." She drew closer and reached out to twine her fingers in Alu's hair. "Or you can come away with me, through the Groves to a place where the gods rest."

Alu's mouth worked, tears brimmed over her eyes.

"I choose my own lovers there, child. You would not come to harm amongst the fairy folk." She tilted her head toward Alu's ear. "Can you say the same for this place?"

Alu just nodded. She licked her lips and cast her eye around the fires.

Fergal remained kneeling, looking wretched, and Kellis huddled under the table.

A great priestess? What I could do to those who wished me harm here.

Her eyes rested on Fintan, his face now glazed in death.

Would I afford them the same fate as Fintan?

"Worship in this world dwindles, child. With every passing season we fade further from this plane. A new god is on the rise, one who is just as cruel to womenfolk. You would be safe among us."

Alu's eyes found Arianrhod's, and in them she saw destiny. Her stormy eyes roiled and flashed and Alu's breath caught.

"Yes," she breathed. "Take me with you."

Arianrhod's eyes calmed to an ice blue, and a smile settled on her face. "You have made the right choice, child. Now, where is the other?" She turned her head to scan the figures huddled in her wake. "Come, Mabh."

A figure hunched over unfolded and Mabh stumbled toward them, awe painted on her ancient face. Arianrhod reached out to cup her face and whispered, Alu couldn't catch the words. She had never known Mabh was also a child of the rites. Arianrhod's hand glowed and light spread across Mabh's skin, coursing over her body.

Alu closed her eyes against the glare. When her eyes fluttered open, a young woman stood in Mabh's place, mouth agape.

"Come, girls." Arianrhod's light grew around her and she was once more transformed into the great white bull. Its head rolled toward its side and Mabh's hand grasped hers. It was Mabh who tugged her toward the beast and hoisted her up onto its back.

Alu held out her hand for Mabh to scramble up behind her, and with a bellow, the bull wheeled from the fires and thundered off toward the Groves.

Alu didn't look back as she left the people of the hills, or when the underbrush of the Groves snapped under the bull's trespass. She knew in her heart she was returning home, far away from the cruel world that raised her. It all made sense to her now, she was ready.

About the Author:

Paula Mason is a writer based in regional Victoria, Australia, who is working on her first novel. She enjoys fantastical stories and faraway places as her creative outlet from her busy day job and (even busier) family.

Along with her first novel, Paula writes short fiction regularly and is the creator of Gretchen's (Mis)Adventures. *This series of novelettes is centred around a wacky witch who is caught in all kinds of fairy tale shenanigans.*

By day Paula is a social worker and has a deep grounding in social justice and child protection. She works within her local Aboriginal community and is keenly interested in reconciliation and restorative justice.

You can usually find Paula on Twitter where she enjoys connecting with other writers and meeting new people. To join in the fun, get in touch @PAMason16. She also has her own website at www.pamasonauthor.com where she talks about her writing process and reading lists.

LORD APIS

BG Hilton

<u>1951</u>

Every night, Sam dreamed of the bull and the sun. Every night, the sun was high above the desert. But in that weird dream way, it wasn't just up in the heavens—it was directly before him, as big and round as a bass drum and shining bright as can be. Sam shaded his eyes and saw that this sun was suspended between the huge horns of a great black bull.

Until this point, the dream was only visual, as some dreams are. There were no sounds and more importantly no sense of temperature. But now the heat struck like a hammer—drier than the Tennessee heat that Sam was used to, but so much hotter.

Sam knew somehow that he was dreaming—that he couldn't die of thirst, not really. It didn't make him feel any more comfortable. He stared in confusion at the wasteland until the bull caught his attention by licking his hand.

"Follow me," it said. It turned and trotted across the burning sands.

There was not much else for Sam to do but follow, his feet sinking into the shifting sands as he walked. Sam couldn't quite make out where he and the bull were headed. He shielded his eyes and wiped the sweat from them, and he could almost his destination, right on the edge of his vision.

But that was always the part where he woke up.

<u>1934</u>

Bobby and Huey weren't burglars, not really. They were warehousemen—or they had been until times had gotten bad. Now they made a living when they could by unloading riverboats at the docks on the Mississippi river. But money was poor and the boats were seldom and, besides, they knew which skylight on their former warehouse didn't open properly.

"You sure about this Bobby?" Hue asked. It was midnight and they crouched on the roof, each trying to raise the courage to open the skylight; each hoping that the other would do the deed first.

"No," Bobby said. "But what else can we do? If'n them boxes for the museum are as full of gold as I think . . ."

"I ain't sure that they are, Bobby," Hue said. "Yer thinkin' them boxes for the museum is full of gold, like King Tut's tomb. But I seen Egyptian exhibitions once or twice. For every ounce o' gold, there's a pound of wood and a ton of clay. What if it ain't nothin' but vases and such?"

"Chance we gotta take," Bobby said. "I can't pay the rent, I'm gonna have to move in with my in-laws in Nashville."

Hue trembled at the words. "Don't go, Bobby."

"You know I don't wanna."

They exchanged a glance in the moonlight and as one they opened the skylight.

"How many times did we tell 'em that this didn't lock?" Bobby said.

"A dozen. Maybe more."

"So it's their fault, really?"

"I 'spect so."

"Then let's do this."

1977

Marjorie Levieux was gradually coming to accept that she knew very little about building works. This was an unpleasant thought, because she had set herself the task of overseeing the remodelling of a dilapidated house in a Memphis neighbourhood on the verge of gentrification. Worse, though she didn't like to think of herself as in any way racist, Marjorie was beginning to under that she found it extremely difficult to defer to the experience of the black builders she had hired.

She felt arrogant and she felt guilty. As with a lot of people, feeling this way just made her more stubborn.

"Thing of it is, Missus Levieux," Henderson the foreman said, "thing of it is, this is very sandy soil. Extending the cellar in the way you want . . ."

"You're going to tell me it'll cost me money, aren't you?"

"Now you're the boss . . ."

"And don't you forget it!"

"Now, you're the boss," Henderson repeated with a sigh. "What if I told you there's a cheaper way to extend the basement? Not by quite as much, I 'spect, nor in the direction you intend, but for much less money."

"How much, then?"

Henderson waved a hand. "None. Say the word, and I'll do it myself right now. Gratis. Won't take more'n ten minutes."

Marjorie frowned. Was she being cheated? Probably, she thought, she was being cheated. But it didn't hurt to ask . . . "How?"

"You see that there wall?" Henderson said. "Different brick from the rest. Real amateur job. I'd give twelve to one that's a later addition, someone wallin' off part of the basement. I take a sledgehammer to that f . . . that false wall, and I reckon I can double your available space down here."

Marjorie's first thought was to accuse Henderson of trying to demolish a supporting wall. But for once, she caught herself in time and just let him do his job.

<u>1951</u>

In Sam's dreams, he was following the bull further and further. After a few weeks, he could see the animal's destination—a city on the shore of a mighty river. The city was built of stone and mudbrick, and dotted with vast temples. The people, brown-skinned and linen-clad, moved silent as ghosts. There was no sound but the wind and no sensation but heat of the sun and the grit of the sand.

It was not an unpleasant dream, Sam supposed. But it confused and disturbed him. Becky, his wife, listened patiently when he told her about it, but couldn't help him understand what it meant. At the studio, Ike was less than interested.

"Dreams, man. What can I tell you?"

"What do you dream about?"

"Fast cars and hot ladies," Ike smirked. "Or hot cars and fast ladies, I ain't picky."

Sam sighed. Ike was, what, eighteen or nineteen? He knew his job, but you couldn't expect deep discussion out of him. "Well I reckon it must mean something."

Ike smirked again. "You know who you should ask? Martha Welbrough. You know, one of the singers on that girl group, uh, the Piretts? Or the Cullottes or some shit. We're recording them Thursday, anyhow. Martha's into talking about dreams and shit. Ask her."

"Maybe I will," Sam said.

"Girls love that shit," Ike added.

<u>1934</u>

"So that's that," Bobby said. The robbery had been a bit of an anticlimax. Before the Depression there been a guard on the warehouse, but in these tough times he'd been replaced by a single man covering four warehouses. Avoiding him had been child's play, even when loading the truck. Now they were at Hue's house, examining their ill-gotten gains. And there had been gold—a little gold, but a little was all they really needed. The rest of the stuff was junk. Probably worth a million to a collector, but there weren't any collectors of Egyptian antiquities in their part of town.

"This one looks like a mummy," Hue said, as they searched through the crates again looking for anything they might have missed.

"Like in that movie with the Frankenstein guy?" Bobby said. "Karloff. That's a face only a momma could love."

"No, not like that," Hue said. Bobby was starting to annoy him. Hue wasn't the most educated guy, and maybe everything he knew about Ancient Egypt came from Readers' Digest, but that didn't mean he wasn't *interested* in the topic. "It's an animal, I reckon," he continued. "The Egyptians didn't just mummify people, they mummified cats, crocodiles, ibises . . . and whatever this thing was."

Bobby looked like he was going to say something ignorant again, but he relented in the face of Hue's earnestness. "Is it a horse?" he asked.

"Could be, it's about the right size," Hue said. "But I reckon it's a bull. The Egyptians used to worship 'em. If there was one that had certain marks on its hide, they thought it was a messenger to . . . uh . . . might have been Ra? Or maybe Thoth? One of them boys."

Bobby shook his head. "You know, if you didn't read so much, you wouldn't be so damn broke. When the Hell are you ever gonna need to know any of that shit?"

"Right now," Hue said. "I need to know right now."

Bobby scratched at his thinning hair. "Okay," he said. "I reckon you got me, there."

<u>1977</u>

"Marjorie, what's up?" Norville Sandersen asked offhandedly, as he poured what was probably his tenth cup of coffee for the day.

"I got a story, Norry," Marjorie said. "A news story."

"Now Marjorie, I don't mean to be rude," Norry said, making no attempt to sound as if he did not mean to be rude, "but you know you're just the weather girl, right?"

Marjorie looked around the newsroom. Rows of desks with hard-bitten newsmen living on a diet of coffee and cigarettes bashing away at their typewriters. There was Wolkowski, thinking no one could see as he slipped a slug of bourbon into his mug. There was Smitty, bellowing into a heavy Bakelite phone while two more phones on his desk were ringing. There was Henderson, swearing at the telex machine as if it might go faster. She had it better than them, Marjorie knew. She was well paid for a much cushier job. Still, she envied those men with their sour faces and stomach ulcers. She'd come into TV to be a journalist, not to point at cold fronts. And here was her chance to be a reporter—even if only for a while.

"I found something in my basement," she said. "You ever hear of the McGregor Collection?"

"Spring or fall?" Norry said.

"It's not to do with fashion!" Marjorie snapped. "Lord McGregor collected Egyptian antiquities. When he died back in the thirties, the Memphis Brooks Museum bought his collection, but most of it was all stolen from a warehouse before it could be catalogued. No one even knows what exactly went missing."

"And it's in your basement?" Norry asked, stroking his moustache the way he did when he was pretending not to be impressed.

Marjorie supressed a grin. "Yes. A bunch of it, anyway. I've opened a couple of the smaller boxes."

"Have you had them checked by an expert?" Norry said.

Marjorie noticed with satisfaction that he'd lost his bantering tone. He was taking her seriously. Finally, he was taking her seriously! "No," she said. "Not yet. But I'll have an expert on hand when we open these crates . . . on live TV."

Norry rubbed the stubble on his jaw. His head shook from side to side and he drew a deep breath. "I'm listening," he said.

<u>1934</u>

Hue's wife, Verna, didn't know about the robbery. At least, that was the fiction. She also didn't know why Bobby and Hue spent so much time together. That way, she and Hue never had to talk about things that neither of them wanted to talk about. So instead, Verna complained about the boxes in her basement.

"Why so many dang boxes down there?" she would say. "Can't move for the dang boxes. Why so many? Huh? Answer me that."

"I told you, I'm looking after them for a friend," Hue would say. He was not happy about the boxes being there, but he also didn't know what else to do with them. The robbery was still in the papers, and Bobby kept nagging him to burn the part of the loot that they couldn't sell.

Hue just couldn't do it. The treasures of Egypt . . . They had survived for thousands of years. Survived invasions and floods, sandstorms and plagues of locusts and whatnot. Their end couldn't come in the form of Huey J. Parson and a jug of kerosene. It just wasn't right.

Besides, Hue kept having these dreams, where the mummified bull was talking to Hue's second cousin, Gladys. Then they'd turn to look at Hue accusingly and a baby would start to wail and the sun would grow brighter and brighter until it was too bright to sleep and Hue would wake up, sweating.

And then one day Hue's neighbour's kid threw out some old Classics Illustrateds—famous stories and novels turned into comics. Hungry for something to read, Hue grabbed them, and in them read a story about a man who walled up his enemy in his cellar. Finally he knew what to do. While his wife was away visiting her relatives, Hue had one last look at his treasures, then bricked them up behind a new wall he built in his basement.

"Tomb for the mummy," he muttered as he fitted the last bricks in place. "Nice dry tomb, surrounded by wealth to take to the afterlife. You remember I did that, Mr Bull. When my time comes, you put in a good word for ole Hue Parsons."

<u>1951</u>

The day before Sam spoke to Ike's friend, Martha, the dream changed again. As usual, Sam followed the bull with the sun between its horns through the desert. Again, he came to the silent city by the river. Again, he walked through the streets between vast monuments and palaces. But this time the bull came to a stop outside a temple. Sam wasn't sure how he knew it was a temple, and he didn't know how he knew he should enter, but enter he did.

Silent and shaven-headed priests bustled to and fro within, carrying on their arcane work. Scribes drew hieroglyphics on the walls. Worshippers silently lay offerings.

At the centre of it all was a vast, imperious figure, as tall as a tree with skin as green as grass. He wore a long, thin, tightly bound beard, like a black rope from his chin. A blue cap adorned his head and a huge golden collar lay about his neck. Other than that the figure was clad in fresh linen bandages, like a dapper mummy.

The giant figure was a god. Sam could feel it. Every nerve in his body was telling Sam to kneel. He pictured his old Sunday School preacher and imagined the disapproval on the old man's face. This image was all that prevented him from prostrating himself before a pagan god.

The god reached out to Sam, who flinched and whimpered. Power, awe and majesty all radiated from the old god like heat off a boiler. But the god did not harm Sam. He just handed him a red and white crown, decorated with a golden cobra. "When you find the Pharaoh," the god said, "give him this."

"Why me?" Sam whispered.

"The bull vouches for you," the god said, with an airy wave of his mighty hand. "And I trust his judgement."

And then Sam awoke.

<u>1977</u>

Marjorie had to concentrate to keep from smiling, grinning, laughing. A big break of a story—and in her own house! Norry had tried to get another reporter to take the whole story, Marjorie had persisted and in the end they'd compromised. Steve Malley would take the lead, but Marjorie would be on screen the whole time, answering questions and pointing things out to the cameras.

Steve was surprisingly okay with this. "Sure it's an exclusive, but it's not my kind of story," he shrugged as the film crew set up. "Honestly, I'm more at home with political stuff, you know?"

"Oh, you're good with the political stuff," Marjorie lied.

"So we're going out live with the evening news, then as a recorded segment on the late news," Steve continued. "We're talking to you, to the builder who knocked down the wall and to that guy from the college, Dr Lionel, whenever he gets here."

"That's right," Marjorie said. She already knew this, having organised it all.

"You open any of the boxes?" Steve said.

"Not a one," Marjorie said. "Figured it was the McGregor collection from the remains of the shipping labels. I remember hearing about the robbery years ago. You'd know about it, if you were from around here. Big deal in local history."

Steve was nodding, but clearly drifting in and out of listening.

"And I've done some research on the house," Marjorie continued, annoyed. "I think the thief was a guy who used to rent this place in the nineteen-thirties, Hue Parson. Former warehouseman, he had an inside track to stealing the collection. He ended up immigrating to Australia in the late thirties."

"Interesting story," Steve said.

"Other than that, the house remained a rental until I bought it," Marjorie continued. "I guess that's why no one did any building work on it. Funny story, for a while in the fifties it was rented by Sam Phillips."

"What, *the* Sam Phillips?"

"Yes. He was trying to get some capital together for his business, so he needed to rent some place cheap."

Steve nodded, finally interested. "Sam Phillips? How about that."

<u>1951</u>

In later years, Sam would realise that Martha was ahead of her time. She was into astrology and tarot and dreams and what have you. She would have been right at home in the late sixties, the seventies. But in 1951 she was just weird.

Even the other girls in her doo-wop group seemed a little uncertain about of her. And she was a little leery about talking alone to a married, middle-aged, white guy—but once he told her about his dreams, her enthusiasm overcame her caution.

"Sounds like Egypt," she said. "Dreams of Egypt are always important. Meaningful."

"Why?" Sam said.

"Cradle of Civilization," Martha said. "Right there in Africa."

Sam shifted in his seat a little at the implication. They were sitting in the mixing booth, which he'd judged as private enough that he wouldn't be embarrassed by bystanders listening in, but public enough that tongues wouldn't wag about him and Martha. "What do you think it means?" he said.

"The bull could be Apis," Martha said. "The messenger of Ptah. That would explain the sun between its horns, he's usually depicted that way."

"Why would I be dreaming of this?" Sam said. "I don't know anything about this stuff. Why's it rattling around my head?"

Martha gave a pitying smile. "Honey, there's more to dreams than just what you know," she said. "Sometimes they're just your mind telling itself a story. But sometimes it's someone else doing the telling."

Sam trued not to shudder as he put out his cigarette—for those were the golden days of shamelessly smoking in poorly ventilated rooms. "So tell me about this bull, Abis."

"Apis," Martha said. "Apis was a messenger, a what-do-you-call-it . . . like a go-between?"

"An intermediary?"

"Yeah, an intermediary. It was this magic bull that was always dying and being reborn. When they found a bull with the right markings, they put it in a temple in the city. It had everything a bull could want—the best stall, the best feed, its own herd of cows."

"Lucky fella."

"Spoken like a man!" Martha chuckled. "When the bull died, it was mummified like a king and laid to rest in a special tomb. Its job was to take the messages of the priests to the god Ptah. Ptah was like a . . . a creator, I guess. He was associated with the sun, and with the Pharaoh."

Sam scratched his head. "The Pharaoh, like in the Bible? The wicked king?"

"Some Pharaohs was wicked, some was good," Martha said. "Many was both."

"That's interesting, but what does it mean?"

"You have any big decisions coming up?" Martha said. "Sometimes dreams, they come to guide us."

Sam lit another cigarette and lit another for Martha. "Yeah, I'm expanding the business. Right now, we just do recordings, see, and sell the masters on to the big record labels. I figure, why do that when I can have my own label? Gonna cost a pretty penny to get going, but I figure it'll be worth it. Had to cut back on a lot of stuff, but . . ."

"But you'd rather talk about that than crazy dreams of Egypt?" Martha smiled.

"Yeah, I guess."

"Well, if that's what you're into, forget the dreams," Martha said. "Forget this new ruler you prophesied, if it's too weird to worry about. But you should take something away from this. I've got an idea . . ."

She grabbed a pen and a pad of paper with the *Memphis Recording Service* letterhead and started drawing something. Sam watched in awkward silence, not sure what the strange young woman was doing.

"You know where Ptah reigned?" she said, after a while.

"Egypt, you said," Sam replied.

"Memphis, Egypt," Martha said. "Here you go. Use this for your new label. Now, I got to get back to my girls before they start talking."

She handed Sam the pad and left. He never met her again, but he did end up using her drawing of the sun as the logo for his new business.

<u>1977</u>

It was lunchtime at Marjorie's house. The camera crew was set up, the news station's van in place, and the expert from the university was looking at the boxes with barely concealed impatience.

Dr Lionel wasn't what Marjorie had been expecting. She'd imagined an old guy with glasses and a white beard, and she was only right about the glasses. The professor was actually a woman in her thirties with long hair, beads and big round glasses. In all, she looked more like she was getting ready to organise a NOW rally than discuss antiquities.

"I can't wait to have a look," she said for the dozenth time.

"Well, as soon as we start the broadcast," Marjorie said.

"I'm just worried about that one," Dr Lionel said. "This big one, here." Dr Lionel pointed to the biggest of the crates.

Now that Marjorie looked, there was something a little strange about it—like the wood had warped a bit.

"Now you say you haven't moved them," Dr Lionel continued, "so that means that this one was right up against where the wall was, here, which puts it right next to your boiler. Heat might have done some long-term damage to whatever's inside. I think we should check it now."

Marjorie was going to say that whatever damage was done, they could wait until the evening news to find out. But Steve looked so bored at Lionel's request, that Marjorie found herself sympathetically interested. "I guess it wouldn't hurt to take a peek," she said.

She looked at Steve, who shrugged.

Dr Lionel grinned and picked up a crowbar. Gently, she eased the front of the crate open. "Oh, wow," she said. "It looks like a sarcophagus for a mummified Apis bull. Eighteenth Dynasty . . . No, I tell a lie. Nineteenth. I wonder if the bull is still inside?"

"One way to find out," Steve said, grabbing the sarcophagus.

Lionel and Marjorie both shouted, as the wood of the sarcophagus crumbled in Steve's hands. The mummified bull within fell to the floor in pieces.

1941

Hue couldn't feel the bullet in his chest. He could see it . . . well, he could see the wound it had left, anyhow. But he couldn't feel it. He couldn't feel much of anything except the sensation of wanting very badly to go to sleep.

He looked around at the chaos and conflict that had seemed so important just a few minutes ago. The other men of his platoon hadn't yet noticed that he had been hit. They were probably just thinking themselves lucky that no bullets from that Stuka had hit them.

That was fine, Hue thought. Nothing wrong with feeling lucky to be alive. Showed you had the right priorities.

The sun was hurting his eyes, so he pulled the brim of his helmet down low, curled up in the desert sand and slept. He didn't expect to wake again. But his eyes opened and the Egyptian desert was empty of Australian troops and German planes and Italian artillery. Instead, there was something much more terrifying: a set of brass scales.

"You understand what is going to happen now?" asked the ibis-headed god Thoth, who had appeared beside him.

"Yeah, I know," Hue sighed. "You're gonna weigh my heart to see if I'm worthy. I read all about it. Reader's Digest."

"'Reader's Digest?" inquired the jackal-headed Anubis. "A book of powerful spells, no doubt?"

"Yeah. In a way. I guess."

"Then let's begin!" Thoth said.

"No," another voice said.

Hue looked around to see a black bull with a white triangle on his forehead and a miniature sun between its horns.

"This one may pass freely," the bull said. "Such is my will."

"This is most irregular, Lord Apis," Anubis said.

The bull gestured with its horns. The other gods bowed and vanished, and now there was nothing standing between Hue and the Lands of the West.

"Hell of a day," Hue said, as he started walking.

<u>1977</u>

The argument between Marjorie and Steve was long and acrimonious, and broken off only by a telephone call from Norry.

"The broadcast is off," he said. "We need the outside broadcast unit."

"Use the other unit!" Marjorie snapped. She didn't usually speak to her boss in this way, but Steve had used up every drop of her patience.

"Damn it, Marjorie, there's no time for this," Norry snapped. His voice wasn't angry though. It was shaky, as if he was on the verge of tears. "The other unit is already . . . already outside the hospital."

Marjorie took a breath. "Hospital? Who died?"

"It was . . . Shit . . . Oh, shit, Marjorie. You . . ." There was the sound of a deep intake of breath as Norry mastered himself. His next words were relatively steady, his voice trembling just a little. "Tell Steve he's gonna need to take his unit down to Graceland."

"Shit," Marjorie whispered. She didn't swear usually. But really, what else was there to say?

<u>1952</u>

Sam hadn't realised he had been looking for the Pharaoh until he saw him. A young man with sideburns, dyed black hair and eyes that could have made a nun swoon. The young man was nothing but a truck driver, but he walked with a swagger and sang with a sneer, and he came to Sam to be signed to Sun Records.

Yes, Sam could feel it. Surely this was he. Surely this was the man chosen by Ptah to be the first king to be crowned in the city of Memphis since Rome was a village.

"So what did you have in mind, son?" Sam asked. His mouth was dry as the desert. The crown that he had been given in the dream . . . he couldn't see it, of course not. But he could *feel* it, like it was right there in his hands.

"I figure a ballad," the youth said. "*My Happiness*, or *Blue Hills of Kentucky*? Or something like that."

"Yeah, we'll record that, for sure," Sam said. "But we'll go with something else, too, something more upbeat. You're a young man, why not something for the kids, something you can tap your toe to?"

"Uh huh," said the youth, clearly uncertain.

"You know Big Boy Cruddup?" Sam said. "He had a song called *That's All Right Momma*. What say we take that, and you put a little rock 'n' roll spin on it?"

The youth gave a smile like the sun. "I know it. It's a good song. Yeah . . . Yeah, I reckon I can do it, Mr Phillips."

The weight of the crown was gone from Sam's hands as he opened the door to the recording booth. "Today, my boy, you're a trucker," he said. "Tomorrow, you'll be a king."

The youth's devil-may-care sneer vanished, replaced by a surprisingly bashful look. "I don't need to be no king, Mr Phillips. I'll settle for bein' a radio star."

No, Sam thought. A king. And you shall have followers and riches and fame. There will be statues of you and paintings; there will be priests and flunkies. And there will be a secure tomb when you die, close by all your worldly riches, but first you shall reign for as long as Lord Apis maintains his power in Memphis.

But he said: "Never settle, son. Always shoot for the moon. Now come on, we're burning studio time."

About the Author:

BG Hilton studied English at the University of Sydney; Writing at UTS, and writes when he's not wrangling his toddler. He blogs about Frankenstein movies, the Leonard Nimoy TV series In Search Of . . . *(aka Great Mysteries of the World) and also writes a free series of rambling soap-operatic spec-fic web stories at bghilton.com.*
You can also find him on Twitter @bghilton.

His short stories have been published in several venues, including Andromeda Spaceways, Antipodean SF, Pseudopod *and in the* Aries *volume of the zodiac series. His first novel, a Steampunk adventure story titled* Champagne Charlie and the Amazing Gladys *will be coming out from Odyssey Books in the near future. He lives in Sydney, but don't hold that against him.*

IF ONLY THEY COULD TALK

Eva Leppard

Barry got home from riding the boundaries later than usual that night. "Bath first," he said to Nance. His boots trailed dirt over the floor.

She glared after him.

He emerged in his terry towelling robe and sat at the table, his meal in front of him. Meat and three veg. Nance knew that it was the least she could do for him, given he'd been outside in the heat all day.

Aussie man, Aussie food.

Barry ate his potatoes. He ate his carrots. He ate his cabbage. Then he laid down his fork and stared at what was left.

The steak sat, massive and glistening. It hung over one edge of the plate, and then out over the other. It was thick. It was medium rare. It was what every diner in every RSL from coast to coast dreamed about.

Premium beef steak.

What else would a farmer have for dinner?

Nance could take even the toughest old beast and transform it into a gastronomic masterpiece. She could cook a perfect steak. She could do a mean rissole. There was nothing she couldn't do with mince. She even, and this had fallen out of favour in the homes of the hoi polloi, (as Nance called them), she even could do amazing things with offal. When she was growing up, a family couldn't turn its nose up at offal. Not in her day. She could whip up a dish of kidneys in red wine that would make grown men cry. She had won awards for her pickled beef tongue. Her commitment to nose to tail cooking was dogged and determined and as ingrained in her as bringing the washing in before the first of the evening dew touched it.

It was what she knew.

It was the most important thing in her life.

But the hero dish was always, always the steak.

Barry's steak was gently cooling on his plate. The knob of butter that had been placed on it ten minutes ago had melted and was dripping off the sides, congealing with the juices from the meat.

"Eat up," she said.

He sighed. A deep sigh. "I don't think I'm that hungry, love."

"Nonsense." She tapped her fork on the edge of his plate, the harsh, tinny sound ringing in the silent kitchen. "Nonsense. You've been out all day. You'll get sick. Eat up."

He stared at the brown mass. Knowing it was a fight that he wouldn't win, he took up his knife and fork.

"The truck is booked to come for the stock in the top paddock then." She knew this; she knew everything that happened on the farm, but sometimes conversations have to be massaged after forty years of marriage.

Barry grunted, all his attention on chewing the hunk of meat that sat in his mouth.

"You'll be bringing them down on Wednesday."

He shrugged nonchalantly.

Nance frowned. "Well you wouldn't want to leave it any longer. They need to be ready to go when Maddocks gets here. We don't have much flexibility. You need to get them out and processed."

"I was thinking," he said slowly, "that we could just hold off on that lot. Maybe just give them a bit longer up there."

She barked out a laugh. "Our bills will be happy to just hold off too will they?"

They lapsed into silence.

"The Bull got in with some heifers," he said eventually.

"How did that happen?"

"Some fences came down."

Nance narrowed her eyes and peered at him over her cup of tea. "Hardly makes a difference now though. They'll have all gone to the slaughterhouse before long."

Barry placed his knife and fork gently on the plate.

Later that night, lying side by side in their cold bed, under the flannelette sheets that did their best to keep out the cold that filled the house, Barry said softly, "Do you think we could try some new dishes? At mealtimes? Maybe we could do something with eggs?"

Nance, who had been close to sleep, turned her head to him. "Eggs are for breakfast."

"I know love, but I was thinking that we could try an omelette. Or a frittata perhaps? For dinner?"

"I'll have none of that in my house, thank you very much."

And that was the end of that.

Barry headed out well before sunrise the next morning. The fence had been brought down by a tree and needed repairing. He wouldn't have known it had happened, wouldn't have gone up there for weeks, if he hadn't seen the lights. The odd green lights. Min lights, they called them.

And then the dreams had come.

He hadn't wanted to go up there, but he couldn't risk this group of cattle wandering onto the rest of the property. Mixing with the other stock. He could have given the job to one of the young lads from town, would have preferred to, but he didn't want anyone else going up there. Didn't want anyone else exposed to what had happened. What was happening.

Anyway, he needed to see it again for himself.

To make sure that he wasn't imagining it.

That had occurred to him, of course, that he had imagined the whole thing. Or that he'd had an attack of some sort, an aneurism or a stroke. But he was certain that he would have felt something if that had been the case. And he hadn't felt something, exactly.

Seen something, yes.

Heard something, absolutely.

The morning sun warmed his back and the motor bike vibrated under him and he knew that this was real.

He stopped the quadbike a few hundred metres from the downed tree and hauled his chainsaw from the back. The scorched circle of earth that lay before him was about thirty metres round. It looked like an enormous branding iron had been thrust into the earth. It was lucky that it hadn't started a fire, he thought idly.

Scuffing the scorched area with his boot, the grass disintegrated into dust and was whisked away by a random eddy of wind, leaving deep circular furrows in the ground. Barry shielded his eyes and looked off into the distance. A line of gum trees; one that had taken down the fence, silhouetted the horizon ahead of him. Clustered along the fence line were a mass of dark bodies, all facing towards him.

Watching him.

Hauling his pack onto his shoulder, lifting his chainsaw, he headed towards them, keeping his head down. He pulled his hat down over his eyes in the hope that he wouldn't attract their attention. Vainly, of course. Eighty pairs of eyes had been tracking him ever since he had walked out of the bush. In fact they may have been here all night, waiting for him to return.

So still.

So patient.

He was close to them now, could smell them; the familiar cattle smell that he had known all of his life. A sweaty, dusty, oily smell. He couldn't imagine a better one. But never had he felt the force of cattle's gaze sit so deeply on him.

The mass parted as he stood in front of them, and as he lifted his eyes he saw the largest, the Bull, walk towards him. The heifers stood back, silent.

"Morning Barry."

Barry licked his dry lips. He should have brought a drink from the bike. How had he forgotten his bottle? "Morning."

"We're glad you came back."

The heifers around him murmured their assent.

Barry took the chainsaw from its case. If he got the main part of the trunk off the fence then he could start repairing it by the middle of the day. He wouldn't get everything finished, but . . .

"How did it go?"

Barry kept his eyes on checking the chain. "It's not that easy. You can't change someone just like that."

There was a gentle chuckle from one of the heifers. "You changed, didn't you?"

"I wouldn't say that. It's all a bit of a shock. And as I said, she's not going to come at it."

"Bring her up here then. Let us talk to her. She will see."

Barry leaned against the tree trunk, arms crossed. "She can't come up here. Her legs aren't any good. And I thought   . . ." He stopped and looked back at the tattoo of marks in the grass. "I don't think that everyone can hear you. Or understand you, at least."

One of the heifers, a smaller one with impossibly long eyelashes, moved forwards. "But you're a start. It has to start somewhere. If they knew that we could think, that we could feel, then things would be different."

The murmuring around them continued.

The Bull looked at him squarely. 'All we want is a chance at life. And that's what they want for us."

Barry cleared his throat and idly twisted a piece of bark off the fallen tree. "How do you know about that anyway?"

The Bull chucked deeply. "We may have only had a voice for a few days, but we've always been aware."

Barry started off into space. "I can't change how the world is, mate."

"Well just change it for us then. We were chosen for a reason."

"What reason?"

"We don't know. We don't know yet. But they've chosen us. And they've chosen you."

Barry dropped his eyes, remembering the dreams, full of lights. "You can't expect everyone to change just like that."

"Maybe you could start farming chicken instead." said the small one again.

The heifers chuckled, a low, rolling sound. "Yes, eat more chicken."

"And sheep."

The Bull swung his head around and they were silent. "We're not asking you to do too much. Just stall things for a while. Please."

"I'll do what I can."

After Barry started the chainsaw, they all drifted away. And by the time he left for the day, to any casual observer they were just cattle, dotted around between the trees and tall tufts of grass.

That night he and Nance had an argument about dinner. He slept in the narrow spare bed, the moonlight splashing in through the window besides him. He started at the full moon, wondering if they were awake, looking at it too. He saw the green lights appear again, spilling their colour over a spot on the mountain. Watching the gentle glow, he slipped into sleep, full of dreams.

"You need to bring those animals down today." Nance slammed his breakfast down in front of him, the massive pile of scrambled eggs quivering. "At the latest tomorrow."

He cast his mind around, wildly. "They're sick." he blurted out.

"Have you got Jim to come and look at them?"

"I don't need Jim to know when we've got sick cattle."

Her lips were a thin, disappearing line. "Well there's nothing we can do then. We can't send them out sick"

Barry shrugged his shoulders. "That's what I've been telling you."

Her narrowed eyes followed him around for the rest of the day.

Early next morning, smiling, she asked him to get a box from the shed that she used for extra food storage. Her legs were worse today, she said. She didn't want to be lugging around more than she needed to. And god knows they couldn't afford a doctor now she said, laughing. The smile didn't reach her eyes.

Glad to be back in her good graces, he swung open the door of the shed, his eyes adjusting to the gloom. He found the tray of tomato preserves on the back wall and was climbing down from the ladder when he heard the door swing shut behind him. The firm thud of the padlock. He beat against the door until the skin peeled from his hands, but he had built a solid shed. There was no way out.

Barry didn't hear most of what transpired that day. The shed was away from the stock yards, but he could feel the low rumbling of the trucks, and occasional yells of workers came to him on the wind. He covered his ears when he heard, faintly, the far-off screaming, plugging them with his fingers and burying his head into his chest. And when the last of the trucks drove away, he heard someone, Nance he assumed, unlock the shed and walk away. He sat in the gathering dusk, on the upturned milk crate where he had spent most of the day, until it was too dark to make out any shapes in the shed.

He could see no reason to move.

That night, when the green lights lit up the mountain, the soft glow growing and becoming a barrage of beams, searching and moving downwards towards the lowlands, Barry buried his head under his pillow and sobbed.

About the Author:

Eva Leppard lives in the bush with her husband, children and a disturbingly large number of rescue animals, many of who she raised by hand whether they liked it or not. For someone who claims never to have enough time to get everything done, she subscribes to a lot of streaming services.
Go to <u>justevastories.wordpress.com</u> for more!

THIS IS THE DAWNING
(PART V)

Helena McAuley

The road had been long, hard, and very dark. It wasn't necessary to drive it, but it was an indulgence in pleasures, a 'last hurrah'. The break at the remote western truck stop was less necessary, again, as was the plate of bacon and eggs with extra barbeque sauce. Bill Riley had loved bacon and eggs, despite his doctor's rebukes. Bill Riley had also loved his job; long-distance haulage. The long days and even longer nights on the roads had given him time to himself, and he quite liked being alone. Breakdowns, flooded roads, and roadkill stuck in axles had afforded him the pleasure of self-sufficiency. In the dark, with nothing but the dim view of the long road before him and the even dimmer view of where he had been behind, Bill Riley had felt the master of his own destiny.

But Bill Riley didn't exist; not anymore.

"When will you be home?" his wife asked through the distorted phone connection.

"A few days," he replied. "It's a big haul."

She yawned down the line. "Remember to get some sleep. And try to eat right for a change. You're gonna see yourself to an early grave."

He only gave a noncommittal hum.

"I'm going to bed. I love you."

He hesitated. "Love you, too." Taurus hung up the phone and returned to his bacon and eggs. It was trying, deceiving Kelly like that—Bill and Kelly had been together for twenty years. They'd had their good times and their bad. The love Bill had felt for her had not been diminished with his incarnation as Taurus, and he didn't want to hurt her. But there were things he couldn't tell her.

Like that Bill was never coming home.

A lump of coagulated eggs fell from the fork as Taurus lifted it to his mouth, slopping onto his shirt. He set his fork down and lifted the spill to his mouth.

"Never developed a taste for them, myself," a lyrical female voice said to him.

Taurus repressed a sigh. He did not look up from the stain. "Hello, Sagittarius."

"I've been trying to keep tabs on everyone," she continued. "At least now I know why I couldn't find you—I was looking in the wrong place. How long have you been incarnate, Taurus?"

He sniffed loudly and looked up. "About two weeks."

Sagittarius gave a low whistle and shook her head. "That must be hard on you. You would have built a whole life by now. What was his name? William?"

"Bill," Taurus said, lifting his coffee.

"What prompted your incarnation?" Sagittarius asked.

Taurus shrugged. "Was just time."

Sagittarius' softly humoured smile lit her turquoise eyes, her auburn hair falling to frame her face as she shook her head. "You're not a big one for words, are you?"

He shrugged again.

"Then allow me to fill the silence."

"No need." Taurus interrupted, loading his fork with more bacon. "Know why you're here."

"Capricorn has found Aquarius."

Again, the indifferent shift of the shoulders. "Good for him."

"You know he'll try to recruit you."

Silence.

"His plan isn't working, Taurus. Humanity isn't ready for this change. This is all happening too quickly."

"Twenty thousand years, Sagi."

"I didn't say it was quick, just too quick."

He shrugged again. "Not really my problem."

Sagittarius watched him with shrewd eyes. Her assessment was met with indifference. After a moment she sat back. "Tell me about Kelly."

Kelly. What could he say about her? It wasn't an amazing tale of love. Kelly and Bill had grown up in the same sleepy little town. Had been sweethearts at school. Bill had left school as early as he could—he wasn't one for academia—and had instead begun driving forklifts for a warehouse and distribution centre. Kelly got a job at the local pub, then the local supermarket, then wherever would hire her. Bill had eventually traded his fork tickets for a truck licence, and the drives became longer and longer. Kelly hadn't minded. She was conscientious and resilient, independent enough to handle the days, sometimes weeks, alone—and this was some of the highest praise Bill could offer anyone. Five years ago, they'd entertained the idea of having children. It didn't work. Kelly stayed, stating she'd only thought about it because having kids seemed to be what everyone did. They'd found out that it was Bill who was shooting the blanks.

Two weeks ago he'd found out why.

The day had been filled with an edgy restlessness. He'd been home for a change. He'd maintained his truck, fixed the broken front gate, fed and clipped Kelly's goats, and tried to work out why the water pump kept stalling. Anything to keep his hands busy. He'd declined an invitation to go down the pub and watch the cricket; he couldn't sit still. He needed to be *doing* something. The restlessness had eaten into the night.

He'd woken with pains in his chest. A tightness and burning that stifled breaths, seized his limbs, and dizzied his head. Kelly was snoring next to him. He'd reacted the only way Bill could—he let her sleep. Cold water on his face and the back of his neck had done nothing to stem the tension. His skin had paled, the black ink of the tattoos on his forearms and chest standing in stark contrast, almost seeming to float above the skin. Panic began to set in. This was a heart attack; it couldn't be anything else. He remembered his dad in the hospital, a once vital man left weak and frail. It had taken months for him to be able to walk down the hallway unassisted.

Bill wouldn't wind up like that.

He took himself into the cold air of the night, staggering steps from limbs unwilling to move. Air no longer making its way to his lungs. His head was noise and tension.

He'd collapsed into the dusty dirt, trembling. This was it. This was the end.

But a part of him *knew* it wasn't. It knew something else...

Every muscle locked as if hit with a current. Joints and sinew strained in an effort likely to tear his body apart. It was overload, it was agony. The breath caught in his chest not even allowing him to scream.

And he *knew everything.*

A thousand lives returned to him in an instant. Glorious triumph, bitter betrayal. Times and places remote enough to be alien to Bill Riley. But all utterly familiar to Taurus.

He rose from the dirt and went back inside.

Kelly was still slumbering, still turned on her side when he crawled back into bed with her. Sleep wasn't required. Not anymore. But he had no other way to spend the hours of darkness, so why not spend them with her? He studied her back, the fall of her hair, the rise and descent of her shoulders as she took breath, the tenor of her snoring. He also felt the tension of the Dawning in the night. It was nearly time, it was nearly here. He would have to go. Not through obligation, or some unfulfilled purpose, but through compulsion. The Dawning was something none of the Twelve could ignore, though he had tried countless times.

Whatever would happen, he knew he wasn't coming back. Not the same, at least.

Kelly's words to him the next morning had shown the extent of her ignorance at his change. *"Geez, you're looking old. How have I never noticed you're going grey?"* Bill had remained silent. *"Well, no more bacon for you, lover. We've gotta start looking after your health. Here, have some porridge."*

Taurus returned to the present. "Kelly isn't your business."

Sagittarius smiled and chuckled quietly. "Fair enough. But at least tell me why all this goosing around with the truck. You could unmanifest and be there in an instant."

Taurus shrugged. "I like the alone time."

Sagittarius smiled again; like she was humoured, like she was familiar. "I can protect you, you know," she told him. "If you'll let me."

Taurus shook his head and wiped his face with a paper napkin. "Don't need protection."

"What can I offer you that will make you side with me?"

He scratched absently at an ear as he contemplated the request. In the end, he merely shrugged. "Nothin'." He lowered the hand to the table. "I'll make up my own mind."

Sagittarius closed her eyes as if restraining herself. Not from violence, but from laughter. "I have missed you, Taurus," she said. "You've been very silent these last centuries."

Again, nothing more than a shrug of the shoulders. "Been here," he said. "Done all this."

"Exactly," Sagittarius countered. "Shouldn't change actually imply a difference?"

Taurus didn't react. Didn't know how to respond.

"I'll see you at the Dawning," Sagittarius whispered and was gone. Unmanifest into the aether.

Taurus sent out an inquiring thought, but only received a gentle acknowledgement. She was gone. A thousand kilometres away. He was alone again.

He stood and retreated to the restroom. Bodily functions, again, were no longer a requirement. But relief was relief no matter how it was expressed. He contemplated buying an apple turnover for the road—Bill would've liked that—then dismissed the idea. Heart attacks may not be a concern anymore, but Kelly wouldn't have approved.

"See ya, Bill!" the kitchen staff called and waved as he left. "Catch ya on the return!"

He waved and exited the truck stop to the sound of a tinkling bell. He wondered if there would be a return.

The crunch of the gravel underfoot was the only sound to break the still night, if one didn't include the ticking and cooling of truck engines, or the fizzes from the mosquito zapper.

Shouldn't change imply a difference?

That was the question, wasn't it? The fated Age of Aquarius, or an Age of Sagittarius. Did it even matter? Would there be a *difference?* Humanity was yearning for change, fundamentally restless, unconsciously bringing forth the Dawning. Humanity ached for equality, for fulfilment, for everything to make *sense*. Both Ages could bring this, in profoundly different ways, but neither would do so swiftly. It wouldn't make a difference to Taurus. It wouldn't make a difference to Kelly. It wouldn't make a difference to their unborn, and forever to remain unconceived, children.

Humanity wanted something *different*. But Taurus feared he had finally become indifferent.

Well, what was it the humans said? Change was as good as a holiday.

Maybe they all needed a holiday. Something to break the stupor.

He reached into his pocket and his hand was met with the jingling of keys.

"Taurus."

He sighed, his shoulders visibly deflating, and turned towards the voice. "You heard, then?"

"Everything," Capricorn said, his burley visage appearing from the shadows. He didn't look pleased. "Is this it? Are you betraying me?"

"S'not all about you, Capricorn."

The older man bristled at the comment, his stubbly jaw clenching. "Sagittarius cannot be trusted," he hissed. "She'll destroy the entire plan."

"Maybe it was a bad plan."

The older man stilled. "Are you telling me you're actually considering an alliance with her?"

Taurus shrugged. "Thinkin' about it."

This time, it was not just Capricorn's jaw that clenched, it was his whole being. A wilful restraint of anger that sent his body into tension. "Taurus," he said, his voice laced with quiet threat. "The plan is all there is. It is the only thing that can save humanity. An Age of Sagittarius—"

"Would at least be different," Taurus said.

That silenced the old man. At least for a moment.

"Humans should be allowed to choose their own destiny," Taurus added.

The returning look was dark with anger. "Humanity cannot be trusted with its own destiny."

Taurus didn't reply. Didn't change the expression on his face. But he was stilled with shock, and perhaps with fear. "Capricorn, I think you've been here too long."

"Don't try to change the issue," Capricorn spat. "Are you with me, or are you against me?"

Taurus shook his head, nodding it in the direction of the truck stop, as if the inhabitants inside represented the whole of humanity. "I'm with *them*."

Capricorn bared his teeth. "So be it." He raised his hand.

Taurus was a moment too slow to react. Couldn't believe he would *need* to react. The burst from Capricorn's emanation caught him in the chest; without restraint, and without defence.

Bill Riley fell dead into the dirt

To be continued in the next edition of the Zodiac Series—*Gemini*. . .

HELENA MCAULEY

About the Author:

Some have commented that Helena McAuley has a pretty good eye for critiquing work. This might be true, with the exception of her own work. And when you find Helena in a sobbing ball in the corner, clutching a bottle of single malt, she will insist she is "Busy editing".
Helena takes her writing as an opportunity to explore her thoughts, such as what does it mean to be human? What is the nature of reality? Is the world interconnected, or is it all just matter and opinion? And how do the cobwebs get in the corner of the ceiling when there haven't been any spiders in the house for weeks?

She has been published in a the ASF Zodiac Series and Stories of Hope *anthology, as well the* On the Edge *anthology and those napkins covered in mindless scrawl that are left at the pub.*

This is the Dawning *is a serialised debut that will be published throughout the ASF Zodiac series. So if you're currently thinking "Woah, Cap! Offside!" then you'll just have to check out the rest of the anthologies to see how it pans out.*

Helena can be found twit-ing, insta-ing, and occasionally facebooked under the handle @thathmc

The author highly recommends readers check out You Have Two Cows . . . *Its old, but still a funny read and a great introduction to political and economic theory. Plus, cows! Moo!*

ABOUT AUSSIE SPECULATIVE
FICTION

Aussie Speculative Fiction is a recently established group which was created to support and promote Australian speculative fiction writers.

Check out our links:

www.facebook.com/Aussiespeculativefiction/

www.twitter.com/aussiefiction

www.aussiespeculativefiction.com

www.books2read.com/rl/asf

ABOUT DEADSET PRESS

Deadset Press is the publishing imprint of Aussie Speculative Fiction—a community aimed at supporting Australian and Kiwi authors. You can learn more at:

www.aussiespeculativefiction.com

ALSO BY DEADSET PRESS

Annual Anthologies

Beginnings: Aussie Speculative Fiction Anthology Vol. 1

Journeys: Aussie Speculative Fiction Anthology Vol. 2

\#

Drowned Earth

Prequel: Shards of Silver by Alanah Andrews

The Rise by Sue-Ellen Pashley

Fire Over Troubled Water by Nick Marone

Submerged City by Austin P. Sheehan

Tides of War by Marcus Turner

The Jindabyne Secret by Jo Hart

River of Diamonds by S. M. Isaac

Salvaged by C.A. Clark

Emoto's Promise by Shel Calopa

\#

The Zodiac Series

Capricorn (The Zodiac Series #1)

Aquarius (The Zodiac Series #2)

Pisces (The Zodiac Series #3)

Aries (The Zodiac Series #4)

Taurus (The Zodiac Series #5)

Gemini (The Zodiac Series #6)

Cancer (The Zodiac Series #7)

Leo (The Zodiac Series #8)

Virgo (The Zodiac Series #9)

Libra (The Zodiac Series #10)

Scorpio (The Zodiac Series #11)

Sagittarius (The Zodiac Series #12)